To Des.

'THE BLUE SMOKE TRILOGY'

and other short stories . . . .

Hope you enjoy some of these stories.

Love,
Grandpa Pinnell

P.S. Keep up the opera singing later

'THE BLUE SMOKE TRILOGY'

and other short stories . . .

by

Dante Cinnell

Press-TIGE Publishing
Catskill, New York

ISBN# 1-57532-165-3

For information:

Press-TIGE Publishing
291 Main Street
Catskill, NY 12414
http://presstigebooks.com
Presstige9@aol.com

First Press-TIGE Edition 1999
Cover design: Drawing Board Studios

This is a work of fiction. Names, characters, places, and incidents either are the product of the author's imagination or are used fictitiously. Any resemblance to actual events or persons, living or dead is entirely coincidental.

Printed in the United States of America

Leading their horses, they came to a narrow rocky passageway which turned at sharp angles and thence into a large cavern. There, the horses were bedded and given roots and tubers on which to munch. The old man bade them to continue on to a smaller cave whose entrance was covered with dry woven grasses. Inside, the radiant warmth of a fire was increased with the hermit's tossing of wood on the dancing orange flames. The grayish black smoke ascended and swirled on the slate ceiling, snaked up an incline and out a crevice in the corner of the cave.

He threw back his black hood and revealed a thatch of snowy, silvery hair to match the beard on the large, craggy face. He offered the men wine, wild grapes and onions, mountain goats' cheese, bread and delectable roots.

After they spoke of whom and what they were, he explained that he became a hermit after participating in many battled, with many victories and a few defeats throughout his years. He tired of war and the burdens of the world and sought the peace and tranquility in Allah's mountain garden of solitude. He asked if they would perform a solemn task on their travels toward home. They would be well rewarded by his friend and cousin, a great sultan in the North. They all acquiesced, knowing full well that they were rewarded already with their lives, warmth, food and drink.

He brought them over to a ledge in the rocky wall where there were many large elephant tusks of intricately carved ivory, depicting battle scenes with elephants and camels. The bases were capped and sealed with burnished banded copper; among them was a sack of copper and silver coins in a leather pouch.

"These," he said, "are for the Sultan of Kabadar, who was kind to raise my only daughter all these years as I fought along the side of his brother who was slain in our last battle many years ago. They are filled with the spoils of war which I have acquired throughout the long years of madness and letters from his long dead brother. They are my debt to him and must be paid before I die. Most receptacles are engraved with words of their contents and a number. Each of thee will carry four treasure tusks, each one different from the others, to be laid at his feet with my eternal thanks and the blessings of Allah. Share the coins equally and take different routes to the Northern Kingdom

BLUE SMOKE

First of the Triology

Many long winters past, in a far away ancient land of wind chimes and sunsets of mauve and deep flame, three mounted warriors were returning home after several years of wars fought in distant lands. They traveled many weary leagues after their army was disbanded, but were now lost in the green gloom of a cold high mountain range. They tried to cross a pass of ice and snow for the sake of brevity in reaching the warmth of their glowing hearths of home.

The friends from the same walled city left together seeking adventure and fortunes in distant lands, but found only the emptiness of war and the premature loss of youth. As they huddled around a small struggling fire to warm themselves in the white, windy, gloomy dusk, their horses dug the snow for meager mountain grasses. Each knew from their experience that nearby death was lurking. They promised each other that should one survive the night and the mountains' hostility, the survivor would visit the families and tell of their fate and love. As their hands touched in bondage over the small windswept fire, each whispered in turn, "Before Allah, I swear my troth."

A dark, hooded figure stood silently among a group of white birch trees watching the young men embrace in farewell.

It was not the Lord of Darkness, but the man of light . . . and flesh. He called to them.

"Young warriors! In this cold and loss of light, wouldst thou share a fire?"

The soldiers drew their weapons at the voice as it approached unafraid through the falling, glimmering snow bouncing up against the hard surface of its frozen brothers.

"Sheath thy weapons, friends, sheath thy weapons. I am but a poor old hermit asking you to share some bread and wine in yonder cave and to save thy beasts from the bitter bite of the northern winds."

The men thanked him profusely, unbelieving of their good fortune surely set before them by the hand of Allah.

of Kabadar to ensure that one or more of thee will get through Corrind, the land of bandits and charlatans."

"I am dying and if all perform this task for me, swear its completion before Allah, as thee swore in the snow before. Thy reward from my cousin, the Sultan, will be great, the contents of each tusk multiplied by the number it bears on the seal."

He put out an alabaster hand. The young men placed their hands on his and swore their oaths. The old man's eyes relaxed and seemed to twinkle as he nodded in trust and took a deep breath in relief of his debt and promise made to his dead comrade.

They returned to the fire and lay on dry, soft branches, leaves and grasses, as the hermit bade them to feed the fire and eat and drink to their fill and contentment. There was comfort in knowing there was more than ample food and drink for this cold and bitter night. They spoke of their adventures, hope and dreams long through the evening's hours as the dark winds howled, piercing the gap between the mountains.

One of the men, a pleasant handsome youth, called Marub Ali, again offered his thanks to Allah and the hermit for his deliverance. Some of the others followed his lead. They were all cloaked in deep sleep as the old man put the last of the large branches on the crackling flames, which lasted until the rising sun shone brightly on the ice hanging from the pines.

When they awoke, the hermit was gone and nowhere to be found. The men loaded the heavy tusks and draped them on each side of their saddles and rear harness. Then the coins were divided equally and they left the cave shouting one last time for the hermit to hear, but only their own echoes reverberated from the mountain walls; then, a great silence reigned among the vast, newly fallen snow.

After descending the other side of the mountain pass the finding the fork in the road, Mustapha, the eldest of the comrades, suggested that they travel together for the sake of safety, since the Northern plains were rife with bandits roaming the land. Chaka, the youngest, agreed but Marub Ali declined, saying that they gave their word to the hermit to approach the kingdom from separate ways to guarantee that at least one of them would succeed in paying the debt owed to the Sultan. They had sworn their oath to Allah and he was bound to keep his word. They parted, Mustapha and Chaka rode the western fork and Marub Ali, alone, took the eastern fork.

In the days that passed, Marub Ali traveled only by night, sometimes walking ahead of his steed, for the animal was hard-pressed with the weight of the payment of diamonds, gold and silver. He purchased a mule to carry the load. The tusks were wrapped in rags of dark brown muslin and put in oblong leather-covered casks to hide their obvious worth from avarice eyes.

Once in the night, he came upon a bandit camp glowing with many campfires and had to sleep until they left in the morning, daring not to venture past their guards near the road, even with the cloak of darkness. When he found towns and villages under the bright canopy of unlimited stars against the dark velvet of the sky, he would wait with his animals and enter at daybreak. His mode of travel and care was laboriously slow but as sure as a giant grinding millstone.

The mule he purchased was to unburden his horse, Jamal, whom he loved dearly. He slept in the stables with his animals, for the amount of coins he had left after his purchase, was down to the weight of ten hummingbirds.

Jamal had once saved his life in battle by staying close to his master where he had fallen wounded, unable to stand and mount his horse. At dusk, Marub Ali, removed his sash and slowly drew it through a stirrup and tied it under his uninjured shoulder. When he weakly rasped the word, "Home," the beast gently dragged his master slowly for half-a-league to his camp where he soon healed under the care of his comrades. From thenceforth, Jamal received twice the excellent care, but no more love in quantity from his master than before, for once a cup is filled, it can hold no more than its walls.

In the second moon of his journey, he passed within ten leagues of his home, yearning greatly to see his mother and sisters, but he continued on. He wished to fulfill his promise and return to work the fields of his mother's farm and lay by the hearth in the evening, playing the flute and being enthralled in the aroma of his mother's cooking. For him, these simple things were now his dreams, replacing in his heart those of his early youth, adventure, glory and riches.

In the last month of his journey, he was forced to seel the mule, his weapon and his saddle, walking next to Jamal the whole way. In his gnawing hunger and pain, he ate grass, roots and soil. He was sorely tempted to break just one seal of one of the tusks, but when he saw, in his mind's eye, the solemn scene of the oath he took to Allah, he quickly dismissed the solution to his increasing woes. Each morning and evening, in his suffering, he would pray to Allah for new strength for his abysmal weakness of spirit and diminishing resolve to keep his word. He was just dust at His feet and did no longer deem himself worthy enough to perform such a task or even to have taken such a solemn oath. It was for men of goodness and fortitude, men of high birth and rank, for holy men of great virtue in much favor with the Master of the Universe, not for the likes of him.

Finally, he, with a slow but dogged approach to the gates of the Sultan's palace in rags and a walking staff, asked in the name of Allah, to have the gifts of payment born and placed at the great Sultan's feet. This was granted, after almost being turned away before he uncovered the richly carved ivory.

The four tusks were laid on the gleaming black marble floor before the throne of the surprised Sultan. He described his quest and his journey from the hermit's mountain. The Sultan, stroking his tufted beard as Marub Ali spoke, intently listened in great amazement as the emaciated, weakened youth spoke haltingly with great effort.

The Sultan had the tusk marked "Diamonds and Ahmad - 1", opened and hundreds of rare blue diamonds of the highest quality gushed out in a spreading cascade of twinkling azure lights. On the surface, were sealed parchments. One written in the hand of the hermit, a second letter was from Ahmad, the dead brother of the Sultan. It was written before he died in battle in time's fading past.

Tears fell from the Sultan's cheeks as the flow of a minute spring freshest from a hillside, as he read both. He sobbed unashamedly twice. When he finished, he put the letters on his breast in his embroidered purple garment.

"By the beard of the holy Prophet, Marub Ali, thou hast done a great service and deed for me and my friend. Thy reward shall be as was promised to you."

"I ask for no reward, my lord, for the hermit has paid me a thousand fold times ten in saving my life and giving me the joyful gift of seeing my family once more. I ask of thee but for a new night lodging until my strength returns and thence continue my journey home. Home to my family whom I have not seen in many years . . . to beg forgiveness for my absence," his voice breaking down at the first mention of home.

"It is given gratefully, but thou will stay longer to gather greater strength. My people have reported that one of thy comrades reaches the palace in less than a fortnight. Then, shall we speak again on his matter. Thou shall rest and wholly regain thy strength. Tonight thou will dine with us with a great feast given in thy honor and for the joy of bringing my brother's words to mine eyes and shall meet the handmaiden for whom thou have born the treasures."

The Sultan ordered his servants to tend to Marub Ali's every need, night or day. That evening among the beauties of feast, music and dance, the maid was presented to him. Her simple, quiet, almond-eyed beauty was great, but her grace and bearing was far greater, the latter part enhancing the whole being. At the end of the evening, Marub Ali deeply loved her and could not sleep as the moon lit his chambers with silvery illumination in the cool summer night. His heart soared when she entered a room, seemingly floating, with her lithe body and smooth gait. Her ebony hair shone in light and in the darkness of the jasmine and honeysuckle scented garden paths. They strolled here each afternoon and evening, providing balm for the wounds of body and spirit he had acquired throughout the years.

In the second week, Chaka reached the palace gates and was received by the Sultan. Again a great feast of fowl, sweetmeats and sugared dates were given. This time the feast was in Chaka's honor for the end of his task.

After speaking with his friend, he related his tale of the journey to the Sultan. He explained how he had to part with his other companion, Mustapha, because of great dangers of thieves, bandits and travel. Mustapha turned back abandoning the task and returning home. But he, Chaka, continued, forced to break the seals of the tusks in order to continue the journey in safety and comfort. He presented the Sultan with duplicates of the sealed parchment letters. The Sultan thanked Chaka for his effort in bringing the letters and the remaining treasure on such a long journey.

When the great hall was emptied, the Sultan clapped his hands twice. The captain of his palace guards quickly appeared, bowed obeisance by touching his breast, lips and forehead and waited for the great Sultan's command.

"Send this day a full contingent of my best men and most loyal and magnanimous officer of the guard, your son, to the City of Marub Ali. There have them find this Mustapha. Let him make a judgement upon the breaking of his oath to Allah. If he has stolen and is squandering the treasurer without good and just reason, have him arrested. Bring him back walking in chains to be put in the deepest dungeon with the empty tusks of his charge. Have your son distribute the remaining treasure to the poor of that city in the name of Allah."

"It shall be done as you command, oh, Most High."

The next afternoon, during yet another day long feast, the Sultan had the tusks brought in and lay on a green velvet coverlet embroidered with fine silver. Marub Ali's tusks were all full, all but one, still with the unbroken seals as they lay at the Sultan's feet. He had each of Chaka's tusks, with the seals already broken, emptied. From the first, his servants emptied the contents onto the green field. Ten pieces of silver lay in a pile, and from the next, forty gold pieces lay in the second. Lastly, sixty glistening blue diamonds in the third; and in the fourth tusk there was nothing.

The Sultan ordered his vizier to have the amount of each pile on the coverlet multiplied by the number on each seal and given to Chaka as his reward. On the morrow when he would leave, he was to be escorted by twenty-two elite palace guards to the very gates of his home protecting his fortune from thieves.

Chaka profusely thanked the Sultan, for he would live in comfort for the rest of his days. He made obeisance to all and started to leave the great chamber for sleep before his journey home the next morning. He promised to inform Marub Ali's family of his well-being, knowing he was requested to stay longer.

The Sultan removed a sparkling collar from his neck on which there were many pearls, diamonds, emeralds and a large sapphire of immense value. This was to be given to Marub Ali's family to sustain them in comfort until his imminent return.

Chaka bowed and was leaving when he stopped, turned and asked, "My Lord, I am most grateful for your generosity and I shall gladly perform this last task, but might I ask the purpose of bringing the last tusk? But for its intrinsic value, I found it empty when in the need to pay my expenses for the journey."

"My young friend, thou are much mistaken," spoke the monarch, "For of all the tusks thou and Marub Ali brought in thy quest, it was the lightest. Yet it contained the most valued treasure of all."

"My Lord, I found nothing. I swear this before Allah."

"Let us see. Break the seal of Marub Ali's lightest unmarked tusk," he commanded.

The captain of the palace guard had two men hold the base of the great tusk upward and he cut the leather seal with his scimitar as all eyes strained to see. When he finally pried the copper seal loose from the ivory, they laid the tusk down and stepped back. Nothing spilled out of the translucent hollow base of the tube. There were no tumbling riches of pearls, rubies or sapphires, nor even expensive rare spices from the south.

Instead, a thick blue smoke eased out slowly and wafted to the spacious domed ceilings, spreading to the arched open windows of the marble balcony. Then it found its way upward among the gentle zephyrs of the indigo night. Like all smoke, it was carried to the waiting heavens and it was gone forever.

"You see, My Lord. Was I not right? There was nothing of value, just blue smoke, was it not?" He said this as he turned one palm up, looking also at Marub Ali for confirmation.

The Sultan tilted his head slightly and gently shook it thrice, as he stroked his tufted beard once more. Then he said in a subdued, yet strong timbered voice.

"No . . . no, Chaka. It was not 'anything' . . . That, my young friend, was 'honor."

After a long pause and silence, Chaka looked down, bowed and, with shame, turned away for home.

THE AGONY OF MUSTAPHA

Second of the Triology

When the hermit of the mountain had commissioned Mustapha and his comrades, Chaka and Marub Ali, in a solemn task to pay a debt in the name of Allah, already had the steel talons of avarice grasped his conscience and spirit, twisting them slowly. He had been duly grateful in having his life saved when lost in the bitter cold and blizzard of the mountain's dusk, but the temptation of carrying some of the hermit's treasure to the far-off kingdom of Kabadar was melting the resolve of the thin bonds of his oath of Allah.

He had been poor all his life, making a living with his family's small grist mill, grinding wheat into flour for the local farmers. His father was paid mostly in the partial weight of the flour finished. He was forced by his father to steal and sequester extra amounts of flour in the grinding process before accounts were settled. The payment of one sack for every score produced, left little for his large family to use in trade to survive. His father had taught him stealing in the frightful task of survival.

When he was seventeen, he married a twelve-year-old second cousin from another city. She came and lived with him and his family. They had a small room in the mill itself.

Great black buzzing clouds of voracious locusts struck the wheat and barley fields, resulting in starvation's large eyes glaring in many windows, in many faces, both young and old.

Mustapha left with four friends for the Land of Spice in the south. Cities at war for rights of trade needed the young to force their wills upon each other. Many caravans from all points of the vast land would seek out the victor and bring much trade and riches. The pay of trained warriors was high. One could fight for much silver and, if he survived the battles and bouts of drunkenness, diseases and dissipations, he could send a few copper coins to relatives to ensure their survival. It mattered not to Mustapha and his friends which city had the righteous claim or which wrongfully coveted of the other's domain. To them, if silver were dropped in their palms at the end of the moon's cycle, then it was right, for their families ate bread and drank milk in a land of want. Justice was disregarded as a bone tossed from a rich man's table to waiting dogs.

When he and his companions left the domain of their savior, the hermit, Mustapha's conscience was in prodigious turmoil in the conflict between his oath to Allah and his greed and lust for riches and survival. That turmoil heightened in intensity when the comrades parted in their ways on the dangerous journey to the north.

If he lost the treasure to bandits, as he almost had thrice, then no one would benefit, so he turned east toward his home and family with the forbidden treasure tusks of the hermit. He would come home a rich man and take care of his family, and as a great warrior should, who but he deserved the reward of spoils of war more? Besides, he could either repay it later when profits were made or he would disperse a portion, albeit small, to the poor in Allah's name.

He lavished great gifts on his family. He provided a beautiful new home for his wife and child, had a new large mill built for his father, acquired slaves for his mother, fine garments and horses for himself, but forgot, or disregarded, the poor. Even though he opened only two tusks, one filled with great gold nuggets and the other with a strange blue smoke, he had spent but one-tenth of the shinny yellow metal. When he opened the silver and diamond tusks, he was in such delight at his good fortune, that the next day he threw copper coins to the squealing children near the fountain where mothers were fetching water in clay jugs. But that was all he did, the poor continued to suffer their deprivations. Just a fistful of copper was tossed only once . . . in the name of Allah.

He enjoyed the life of a rich man for four moons, when forty-one mounted-horsemen from the Sultan of Kabadar appeared with flaming torches and, by the dim lemon-light of a partial mood, dragged him out of his bed and into his new scented gardens. They clamped chains to his ankles and wrists and removed the treasure tusks from his locked vault. The next day its contents were to be distributed to the poor of the city. In the blackness of the star-filled night, Mustapha was led away married to the chain which would be his first mistress for nearly a lifetime of agony, shame and solitude. The Sultan of Kabadar was a stern taskmaster in his servitude to the justice of Allah.

For eighteen winters, Mustapha was tethered on the long chain of the Sultan's wrath in the deepest, darkest dungeon of the opulent palace. On the opposite side of the dark gray walls, hung the four empty tusks of his charge to remind him of his treachery. From one, a dark blue smoke leaked out slowly and snaked its way to a high barred window to the freedom denied to the wretched prisoner.

Through the many bitter years of cold nights, he had prayed to Allah for release, then for death, and finally forgiveness. He prayed many times during the long nights, for the glaring gift of the hot sun was denied to him as was the light of God.

All his prayers now were for forgiveness, for he, as a boy, had listened to stories of holy men speaking in the marketplace by the full of the moon; he heard that Allah's justice was all-encompassing and something to be feared but also His mercy was unbounded. As the intensity of his prayers of entreaty for forgiveness increased with no thought of freedom, so did the thickness of the blue smoke from the single tusk. At the height of the moon's silver fullness, it shone into the dark dungeon illuminating the thickening, slow-easing smoke with an illuminating glow where Mustapha could see his hands, beard and chains in its radiance. Finally, he prayed only to the greatness of God, no longer begging for forgiveness.

In the nineteenth winter, the old Sultan was relieved of his dire infirmities by the Lord of Darkness, but there was no similar kindness extended to Mustapha. But for the new jailer's porter, taught to bring food and drink to the dungeons and to descend down circular steps of cut stone to the one deepest in the palace, all had forgotten Mustapha lost in the abysmal darkness below.

The new Sultan, Ahmad the Second, was declared Caliph of the five sultan ships of the north. He commanded a vast army, mighty argots of war and trade, vassals, two score of magnificent palaces and four hundred wives and concubines. He was loved and revered by his people as their new, great king, but was a humble servant to Allah. Yet with all his power, glory and obeisance paid to him, he felt as the lowest beggar in the land.

One of his children, a diminutive girl, was born with a deformed leg and foot. She captured every heart who knew her with her cheerfulness and forthrightness. Her only complaint was that she could not run and play with her siblings and cousins. She would sit by herself for long periods when her mother and father could not attend her.

Although her happiness was innate, Ahmad loved this child so dearly that he would have gladly traded all he owned in an instant for her wholeness, although she herself was happy.

Ahmad was an advocate of Allah's mercy more than His justice, so on the day of his coronation, a Caliph of the Five Kingdoms, he proclaimed amnesty to all those imprisoned, whatever their crimes except assassins. Prisoners were to praise God and start life anew. The following day, messengers and hundreds of carrier pigeons sent his edict to the far corners of his kingdom. He lead a coterie of nobles to the dungeon areas and had the jailers open the heavy oaken doors and provide silver to prisoners who filed past. Some groveled at his feet and kissed his garment, but he only said, "Give thanks to Allah for his mercy and praise his goodness."

The jailers, however, had forgotten about Mustapha, for he was condemned to the lower tier, where none ventured. The fourth porter had died a month before and the new one, uninformed, had not fed Mustapha. He survived by licking water trickling between stones and devouring, when he could, insects, salamanders and rats.

When the group of nobles was leaving the upper tier of the dungeon area, dooming Mustapha to a slow death by starvation, one of the young nobles, noticed and pointed to the blue smoke coming from a dark stairwell.

Ahmad asked, "What is down those steps?"

After a quick conference of the five jailers, one said, "A dungeon, my Lord."

"Is it occupied?"

"No, my Lord Ahmad, it is reserved for, I was told, for traitors. I have been here in thy father's service for fifteen years and no one has been put in there in all that time."

"Then where does this smoke come from?"

"I know not, my Caliph."

"Let us go and see. Lead the way."

The five jailers bearing torches, descended the circular stairs to the great door of the last dungeon, where a barred window looked down the last set of steps. As the Caliph peered into the gloom with some of his entourage, an older jailer remembered and said, "Mustapha, sire. Mustapha! Now I remember. Thy venerable father condemned him for breaking his oath to Allah and stealing the treasures of repayment. It is he, my Lord, it is Mustapha!"

When Ahmad peered in again, his dark brown eyes shone great pity. The wretch below was in deep prayer oblivious to the many eyes above him. Ahmad gave a quiet command to his guards, "Free him."

The heavy unlocked door was pushed open by four men. The guards descended the murky steps carefully and as their boots noiselessly sank in the muddy slime, Mustapha was finishing his prayer of praise. The captain of the guard swung his broad scimitar with a mighty blow and severed the rusty eroded chain from the main link in the stone.

Mustapha was startled by the sound and the sight of strong arms and hands lifting his frail body to his feet. Although s hrunken in height throughout the years, he was still a hand taller than the guards. His wretched filthy frame was laid at the feet of Ahmad. His eyes were blinded by the glare of the torches like a hundred suns, he raised an emaciated forearm to cover his eyes because he still could not see.

"Art thou the man called Mustapha?" said the Caliph.

The kneeling form nodded and replied in a labored slow voice, barely audible from the lack of use for so long.

"I...am . . . Mus, . . . Mustapha," he said as his head dropped to his chest.

A noble asked, "The one who broke his oath and stole the treasure of the Sultan many years ago?"

Mustapha nodded twice, for speech came too hard, although he was surprised in its function.

"From this day forward, Mustapha, thou art free," said Ahmad.

"Sire, if I may dare to oppose the Defender of the Faith," said his vizier, "that your departed father wished him to serve the sentence for life."

Ahmad pondered briefly. "And so he shall, but he will serve his penance as a freeman."

Mustapha did not respond as his head shook trying to discern the faces which spoke the strange words which his brain refused to understand. The words "freedom" and "free" were almost long forgotten as words or a state of being. He tried to repeat the words but could not. Only four words flashed repeatedly across his mind.

"Praise be to Allah!"

"Have him tended to," said Ahmad. "When he has recovered sufficiently, bring him to me."

* * *

In the weeks that passed, Mustapha partially regained his strength and vigor and was brought to the Throne Room where he once was condemned by the old Sultan. He walked with a bamboo cane and wore a shift of soft white cotton tied at the waste, pantaloons of the same material and a turban of white to reflect the hot sun during the many days of recuperation. He bowed deeply and dropped to his knees and touched his forehead to the black marble floor in thanks to this great king for his mercy.

"Well, Mustapha, it is time for thy freedom. It is at hand."

"Great king, I thank you and Allah for the great undeserved mercy bestowed upon me from the punishment decreed by thy father, the Sultan."

"Was his judgement on thee just, Mustapha?"

"Verily, it was, Lord."

"And thee hold no animosity on his decree?"

"None, my Lord. I should have been put to death for my crime, but through thy father's instrument and thine, perhaps Allah can forgive the reprehensible acts I have committed. I wish I could make amends."

"You can, Mustapha."

"How Sire? Just command me to perform a penance and it will be done. I swear true this time."

"So be it then. To test your new honor, you will roam the

vast land from corner to corner with the same tusks of thy charge, refilled with treasure to be dispensed to the poor and needy wherever thou find them. When they are empty, they will be replenished as need be. Thou will roam the land for a score of winters. Will thou accept this task and swear before Allah again, for this time if thy word be false, thou will return to your dungeon again, never to leave. Take care not to swear falsely."

"My Lord, I swear again before Allah to perform this penance, completely, but may I ask that in my journey, I may visit the city of my family to see what has become of them?"

"See them and care for them in any way thou wish, then continue thy task to its completion as a merchant. Mind eyes and those of Allah, will follow thee."

* * *

So began Mustapha's penance. With horse, three mules and four tusks, he traveled incognito as a merchant of pottery and cookware. When he reached a large city, he would stay for many days, seeking out the needy, the poor, the blind and the lame, greatly assisting them surreptitiously. He appointed a trustworthy, holy man to oversee a large fund left with merchants for profits, from which constant interest and profit would be available for many years for their care and well being and, in some instances, financing their cure. When all was done, he would move on to the next village or town.

Three years had passed until he finally arrived at his own city, with high walls of protection against bands of bandits, of which there were many. After administering much help and succor to the needy and the afflicted, he sought out news of his family. In his long imprisonment and travels, he found that suffering a score of years in waiting, his wife had to remarry to support her children, after hearing rumors of Mustapha's death in prison. Although she did not love the shopkeeper who courted her, he was a good man whom she grew to love, as he was kind to her and her children. Mustapha's four children had since grown, married and had children of their own. He had eighteen grandchildren.

He learned his family lived near each other by the grist mill of his deceased parents. Most of them came to the Wellspring of Allah's Tears to carry water for their needs and many of his younger grandchildren would play there in the square.

On his land day, he visited the well. He distributed copper coins to all of the children and asked their names, learning which of them were his grandchildren.

"Are you a rich merchant?" asked one little boy.

"What is your name, boy?"

"Mustapha," he answered.

"Well, Mustapha, in a way. Like most men I am very poor and in another way, I am very rich."

"You must be the richest man in the world," stated a small girl standing next to little Mustapha.

"And what is your name little one?"

"Sariman," she answered.

"Ah, Sariman . . . a very beautiful name. You must be named after your grandmother. No Sariman, I am the poorest of men."

A man and an older woman approached the group near the fountain.

"Father, grandmother, look what the rich man gave us," each child showing them a silver coin.

The man looked down at their palms as he filled an earthen jug with the clear water. Mustapha's eyes drank in the sight of his son and wife.

"You are too generous, stranger. I have heard you have given much to the poor. Why do you do these things?" he asked.

"I do nothing but give in Allah's name as He commands," he answered.

"My mother and I thank you, stranger. I would be pleased if you supped with us at my humble home this evening," he said.

"A thousand thanks, but I must now begin a long journey," he said mounting his horse. He looked long into the man's face and that of the old woman. He then spoke to the little girl, "If thou want to see one of the richest men in the world, little Sariman, look to thy father. May the peace of Allah be showered upon you all. Goodbye." He then lead his train north to Kabadar without looking back.

* * *

Outside the garden of the palace, he sat on a stone facade as he waited with his horse and mules, to report to the Caliph of his task and to replenish the treasures in the four tusks. The Caliph's grandchildren were running and hiding among the many different colored roses and jasmine bushes. A beautiful little girl of four with a clubbed foot limped over to where he was sitting and sat watching the raucous games of her siblings and cousins.

"What are your animals' names?" she asked.

"My horse's name is Jihad. The mules have no names, little Princess," he answered.

"Oh, they should have a name also. Otherwise how will they come to you when you call them for supper?"

"You're very wise to have thought of that. I have had so much trouble calling them. I never thought of that. Why don't you name them for me, Princess. I would be eternally grateful," he said.

"We can call the first one Jasmine and the second one Blue Rose and the third Pink Rose," she said as her black eyes twinkled in delight.

The Caliph approached with his retinue. He picked up his daughter as all made obeisance and hugged her warmly. She stroked her father's short beard with affection as he sat on the wall with her. She was the only one who dared to do such a thing. She only thought of the Caliph as her father and nothing else.

"Father, I have named the horses. That's Blue Rose, Pink Rose and Jasmine," she beamed as she pointed with pride.

"What beautiful names, Mahala. Did you think of them all by yourself?" he asked.

"Yes I did, Father," she answered as she stroked his beard again. He loved her diminutive hand with her soft touch.

"Sit, Mustapha and tell me of your good works."

As they spoke, the blue smoke from the empty tusk on Pink Rose's back cascaded slowly down to the ground. It slowly rose to Mahala's foot and leg and hung there even though her leg moved about on her father's knee. The Caliph noticed it and waved it away, but to his amazement, it again clung to her leg as a soft blue beneficent fog.

"No my Lord, let it be. I beg you," asked Mustapha.

Soon the smoke dissipated. To everyone's amazement they saw the Princess's leg was less crooked and her foot was less bent under her weight. She walked much better and could even run a little back and forth, as she yelled and laughed with delight.

"It is the hand of Allah, Mustapha," said the Caliph as tears welled in his eyes. "I can never repay you. Ask of me what thou will of all my possessions and it shall be yours, anything. And thou art free, Mustapha, of thy penance. Allah has shown that. Thou art free, thou shall be rich beyond your dreams and thou can return to your home and family," he exclaimed jubilantly.

"My Lord, I am most happy for you and the Princess in Allah's benevolence, but I have no wish to be rich. I am now alone in this world. I ask that I be allowed to continue what I am doing. For I have never been more fulfilled than I am now. Delving out your gracious gifts in the name of Allah brings me unbounded happiness more than perhaps any man has ever known. Just let me continue my work."

"So be it then. Go Mustapha, my friend, messenger of Allah."

KAREEM, SON OF CHAKA

Third of the Triology

When Chaka returned home, he was well met by his family and friends. The retinue of the Sultan's palace guards had escorted him and the remaining treasure to his very door, then parted quickly refusing half-hearted hospitality. His wife and two children were pleased to see him after the long hiatus as a soldier.

His son, Kareem, was now fourteen and his daughter, Balisaad, was thirteen. After a few weeks, the family moved into a great house with a garden and high walls.

He told of Mustafa and Marub Ali's duplicate tasks in the same quest, but did not mention the differences in their efforts. His wife told him of the arrival of Mustafa just weeks ago and how he too brought home great riches and acquired a new home and grist mill for his parents.

Chaka recounted the journey home from the wars and how he had acquired the riches from the Sultan of Kabadar, himself, in a long, dangerous and tedious mission to pay the debt of the old hermit of the cave.

Chaka's wife told of Mustafa's arrival, also opening all the tusks and he could not understand carrying such smoke needlessly all the distance. He would seel the tusks after he emptied them of the spoils, or perhaps keep one as a reminder of his good luck in acquiring his riches, she explained.

"What does it mean?" Chaka's wife asked.

"It means that the Sultan's palace guards might arrest him for stealing the treasure and breaking his word to Allah, unlike me, who endured great hardships and deprivations to keep my word, my bond. There will be no soldiers of the Sultan come knocking on my door," he boasted.

Chaka went to visit with Mustafa at his new home and told of how he completed his journey to the Sultan's palace and how he met Marub Ali there and how he was rewarded tenfold for his successful effort in the task. He had more riches than Mustafa who did not complete the mission. He told of the strange blue smoke emanating from one of the tusks but offered no explanation.

"I too saw this smoke in one of my tusks and still it issues forth, though lessened," explained Mustafa, "but the tusk, itself of carved ivory from Cathay, must be worth thousands of rupees. I shall sell it for the highest bid at the bazaar of Ramadan when next I attend it, then buy a score of slaves."

"Mustafa, my friend, I would consider moving your family to a distant land soon should the Sultan be vengeful. When I left Kabadar, there was talk in the marketplace that the Sultan was seeking you out for punishment. I am surprised they have not yet come."

"What punishment can there be? Did he not receive the contents with your delivery and Marub Ali's? Was the hermit's debt not paid? I could no longer complete my journey without great risk to my life and then, only bandits would have gotten the payment and my family would have starved. Where is the justice in that? My family comes before all things, even Allah. Besides, in all this time that has passed, nothing has happened."

Chaka stood in his rich robes from the silk cushions and said, "My friend, I do not make judgement on your decision. I only warn you of the talk. Now I must go and I must deliver a gift to the family of Marub Ali and tell them of his well being. Then I too, am buying a new home and slaves for our comfort."

Within a fortnight, soldiers came to Mustafa's new abode and arrested him. On orders of the Sultan's officer, the soldiers then dispersed the remnant of the treasure, great amounts of gold and jewels and to many holy men to disseminate among the poor of the city. Then he was taken away in chains with his tusks.

When Chaka went to see for himself, he spoke to the young officer giving to the poor in Mustafa's now empty house and asked about him.

"He is back to Kabadar. You may see him before he departs with us if you wish. We would have been here sooner but were delayed. We assisted in defending an attack by many bandits on one of the Sultan's caravans."

When the officer dispersed all the gold, he mounted his dark steed as his contingent appeared on horseback leading Mustafa walking behind bound in chains still wearing rich garments.

He and Chaka looked at each other, both disbelieving.

"Take care of my family, Chaka, I beg you as a comrade."

"They shall not starve, Mustafa, that I promise you."

* * *

In the years that passed slowly, Chaka no longer provided for Mustafa's family. They were getting along on their own. Why should he when he had to care for his own? Mustafa had his chance, he thought, just as he and Marub Ali did. Was not Marub Ali now a powerful lord in the south after marrying? Luckily, he had substituted a diamond for a bejeweled collar to be given them from the Sultan. They did not need it, since Marub Ali provided grandly for them. Besides, his daughter was about to be married and the expense would be formidable. Two great problems with his increasing riches were that he needed more, and that his son wanted none of it. Kareem was a somber youth who read constantly and spoke to the wise men, astrologers and soothsayers for hours at a time. He was not interested in his father's investments in merchant ships to the Spice Islands to the west, nor the lending of money to other merchants for profit or long caravans to Cathay and Persia.

Chaka had become so rich that he needed a score of accountants and scribes to keep track, yet he paid little in wages and gave nothing to the poor and widows in the name of Allah's mercy. The treasure chamber deep in his great house was full. As a child, Kareem would play pirate and bandit chief in the great room illuminated by the least of sun rays from above, yet the whole chamber would bask in the false aurora from the gold and diamonds' reflection. The strangest object he found to play with was a great carved elephant's tusk from which emanated a trickle of thick blue smoke. He imagined the smoke was a powerful jinn, his to command for every whim. He never asked for riches, for there would be no more room in the chamber, so in his mind's eye, he had his genie take him to the far reaches of the world, to the highest mountain tops, to the bottom of the great salt seas, to the purple firmament among the sweeping stars of night, and to the gates of Paradise, but he and his jinn were forbidden to enter. When they looked in, they saw many happy people, children playing, talking, walking among perfect hills of green and meadows. Many were lying about jabbering happily outside colorful tents, roasting tidbits of lamb among small campfires. Kareem looked at Allah, hoping to catch a glimpse of the Master of the Universe. He imagined him to look like his soft-spoken, kind grandfather who died.

Soon the fanciful vision faded, the genie dissolved and escaped; all that was left was the cold, lifeless gold. He wanted so badly to see his grandfather whom he missed dearly.

As years rolled by, Kareem became a reticent youth who cared little for the opulence of his father's house and possessions, although he worked tirelessly for him. On his own time, he would walk the city, giving beggars and children coins. He knew that some of the beggars were not blind or lame, but he gave anyway on the chance that he was wrong. He sought out experienced men talking in the bazaar and listened for words of wisdom. He'd sit at the marketplace at night as the storyteller wove his web of high adventure, of magic and genies, of the travels and exploits of Sinbad, of gargoyles and wizards, and of lands in far away misty seas where there were giants and pygmies warring. Only one poor dying sailor returned to tell the tale.

Months passed as Kareem, the young man, grew more restless. His sister, Balisaad, was married and given an adequate wedding. Chaka insisted he'd only pay for half the expenses. She and her new husband left for Bhasra where he owned a shop selling rugs and pottery. Kareem gave them a fine gift which cost all the money he had earned through the years working for his father. Chaka begrudgingly gave a small gift, saying that he paid for half the wedding and that was more than enough.

* * *

One dark night, as he listened to more stories by the storytellers, soothsayers and wise men, he heard the story about his father and his friends returning home from war as young men and being lost in the mountains in the cold grasp of winter.

"They were saved by a wizard and each given a task of honor to perform in the name of Allah," said the storyteller. "Each soldier went separate ways to pay a great debt of honor to a great sultan. One performed it with great hardship in travel and nearly died. He was rewarded handsomely and became a prince in a far distant land. The second absconded with the treasure, but was caught by the Sultan's soldiers and imprisoned for life with both hands cut off. The third spent most of the treasure and was rewarded little by the Sultan and is now a beggar for bread and coins in the streets of Kabadar. All but one brought the wrath of Allah on their heads."

Kareem stood up from his sitting position in the darkness and yelled, "No! Allah is all merciful! He forgives all transgressions. It is true that one became a prince, and deservedly so; the second soldier who stole the treasure was forgiven by the Sultan's son years later and now, with his help, roams the land giving aid and alms to the wretched in the name of Allah."

"And the third?" yelled a voice in the darkness.

"Why, he is no beggar, but one of the richest merchants in the land," Kareem answered.

"Then there is no justice, for he has escaped Allah's punishment."

"No, he has not!" replied the youth. "For although he is the richest of the rich, he is the poorest of the poor. I know . . . because he is my father!"

Then Kareem exited in the darkness among the murmurs of the crowd. In the opposite direction, Chaka left with tears in his eyes.

* * *

An important caravan was set to go across the mountains to Cathay. The caravan master became ill and died two nights before it was to leave. Chaka asked that Kareem lead it since he had made that journey twice as a youth. He knew the terrain and the pitfalls better than anyone in the city. They hired another caravan master to assist him, but he insisted to bring his small son along as there was no one to tend him. They left on schedule as a red dawn broke against the hills and pink sky in the east. Kareem lead it with his father's best black stallion.

In the weeks that passed, Kareem and the boy, Abu, became friends. The boy's black eyes beamed with delight as they reflected the campfire's light as Kareem recounted some stories he knew from the marketplace. When Abu's father checked the guards at night, Abu would sleep in Kareem's tent.

One night a small sand viper crawled in under the flap and bit the boy on the leg as he turned over on the snake. Kareem awakened suddenly and killed it. He took his jeweled dagger out quickly and cut into the screaming boy's calf. He sucked out all the liquid he could and spat it out. He cut into the wound again without hesitation and squeezed and sucked more fluid out, but he knew it might not be enough. A man perhaps could overcome the effects of the remnant venom, but a boy could not.

As the boy went into a feverish coma, a camel driver told of a doctor in the city below the hills. After directing his father to follow with two camels to ensure his arrival, Kareem scooped up Abu on his stallion and rode at a full gallop toward the city. He was directed to the doctor's abode, where Abu was tended to with medicines and herbs, which helped but slightly.

"There's nothing more I can do. The rest is in the hands of Allah," the doctor said.

"But surely we can do something else. The boy is so small and frail. Perhaps a cool bath to bring down his fever."

"I doubt it, but we can try," said the doctor. "There is also the possibility of . . . "

"What? Please tell me!" cried Kareem.

"There is a hermit who comes down from his cave in the mountains to trade and tell stories. They say he is a great healer. He sleeps now, where he always sleeps when he comes down, in the stables of the Inn of Paradise's Gate."

"Have your servant show me the way, please, and I will get him. I will pay ten times your fee if the boy lives!"

* * *

Using the doctor's medical cart, Kareem returned with the hermit and the servant. The old man in the black hooded cassock and walking staff came unhesitatingly after Kareem told him of the boy's plight. He removed his hood revealing a thatch of snowy hair and icy beard. He looked long at the quivering boy in the dim yellow candlelight without saying a word. Then he reached out with a frail, almost alabaster-colored, hand and placed it gently on Abu's forehead, then with the other hand. Both slid lightly to the temples and softly cascaded to the cheeks, neck and chest with the thumbs resting on the boy's rapidly beating heart. His touch was like the touch of hummingbirds on a lily. More long minutes passed as Abu's quivering and breathing eased.

"Why, this boy is not ill," announced the hermit. "He's probably just tired from too much play. He'll be all right in the morning. Let him rest the night."

"Too much play?" queried Kareem, "Grandfather, he was bitten by a sand viper!"

"Perhaps it was a young one then," said the hermit covering his head and his soft craggy features melted with beneficence into the shadows.

The doctor checked the boy and nodded his head saying, "Yes, the boy will live."

Abu's father burst in and was told what had happened. He

buried his head gently in the boy's neck, sobbing and thanking all and thanking Allah for His mercy.

The next morning Abu and his father left on their camels after Kareem gave orders and instructions to complete the journey of the caravan. He was staying to follow and learn the ways of the hermit.

"But, Master," he said, "what shall I tell thy father?"

"Tell him what I told you and tell him if he wants to be happy, to give away his riches to the poor and go live with my mother in a little hut by the Lake of Willows to live out their days in contentment. I will visit them as soon as I can," he said as he smacked both camels on the rumps yelling, "Hut, hut, hut!"

* * *

When he arrived at the inn, he found the hermit had left. When he asked the porter which direction, he pointed to a snow-capped mountain range to the south.

"How will I find him?"

"Master, he only left at sunup and there is only one road toward the mountains."

Kareem galloped away hoping not to lose the hermit. In a short time, he caught up to the dark hooded figure who looked back to give way, but the horse never passed him as Kareem dismounted and walked with him.

"Grandfather, I wish to follow you and learn your ways. It's what I always wanted, although I never knew it. Please let me journey with you grandfather," he beseeched.

"What is there to learn from me? Do you seek magic, tricks and illusions? I know no magic, use no tricks, hold no illusions. I live a lonely life in peaceful solitude in my cave with some small animals, a few mountain goats for milk and cheese, wild grapes for fruit and wine and sometimes a warm fire on a winter's night. I wake with sun and sleep by the moon. I read only the Koran and pray six times a day facing Mecca, no more nor no less than the simplest of men. I even pray as I walk. What can I teach thee that thou dost not already know?"

"Teach me to heal. You healed the boy."

"I did not heal the boy. I simply prayed to Allah and He healed, if that is what you wish to call it."

"Then, please, Grandfather, teach me to pray as you do so Allah listens."

"Any child can pray and Allah listens. The secret, if there is any, is in the heart, sometimes because of purity, sometimes because of sin, or the forgiveness of sin. Who can tell of the mind of the Master?"

They walked with the stallion clopping behind Kareem as gently as a family dog.

"He must listen well to you."

"Kareem, do you want a life of loneliness? It's that which most people fear the most in life."

"How did you know my name? I never mentioned it."

"I don't know. The boy's father might have mentioned it. Is it loneliness you want, boy?"

"I have a family and a few friends," he said, "yet, I've been lonely all my life. I have been seeking something, something intangible. I never knew what it was. Grandfather, until I saw with my eyes what thou did with thy hands. I want more than anything to help people as thou do."

"If there were such a gift which could be given or taught, the price would come dearly, I'd imagine. Would thou be willing to pay such a high price in suffering and denial of comforts of the flesh?"

"Yes, Grandfather, I would."

Just then as they rounded a small bend on the dirt road, they came upon an old woodcutter, trying futilely to pull his cart from a shallow ditch where his donkey had stumbled and died of old age. He had two small children with him trying to push the solid wooden wheels up the small incline. The children were dirty, undernourished and dressed in rags.

"Masters," said the frail old man, "would ye help in the name of Allah. My grandchildren cannot help enough except to help me pull the cart to the city. There was no one at home to care for them. Sirs, I beg your help in getting the cart back onto the road."

The hermit started to grab the harness to pull when Kareem yelled, "Wait, Grandfather!"

He took the harness and ran it through the stirrups of his saddle, secured it and let his horse away from the heavily laden cart. It pulled up in two strides of the gentle stallion. After a few bows and many thanks, the old man and the children secured the harness around their shoulders and waists to begin their arduous journey to the marketplace.

The hermit sat on a grassy bank with his walking staff on his lap intently watching the episode in silence.

"Wait, Grandfather," said Kareem, "We have not finished." He took the harness from them and again secured each side to both stirrups, put the children on the cart and handed his jeweled dagger to the boy. Then he handed the old man the reins of the stallion, patted the horse's head and gave him a hug.

"Take him, Grandfather, he is yours. Take him to the doctor's house and have him sell this horse and dagger to the richest man in the city. With the money, you can buy a hundred donkeys and the jewels in the dagger will take care of your grandchildren for a long time. The old man was stunned into immobility and speechlessness. He looked with tears in his eyes at the hermit for validation of the act. The hermit merely gave the smallest of nods and a slight smile as he closed his eyes slowly. As they started to lead the stallion away, Kareem ran up to the cart and placed a leather pouch containing gold and rubies into the girl's hands and caressed her filthy face."

They watched as the cart disappeared around the bend with the children looking back not understanding what was happening.

The hermit got up and began to walk toward his mountain as Kareem joyfully took up along the side of him without a word, but his heart was bursting with joy and he was smiling beyond control.

"And now a new journey for you," said the hermit without looking at him. "A long hard journey indeed, Kareem, . . . son of Chaka."

ALBA OF THE MOUNTAINS

She was only about sixteen in 1924, but already flowering into a truly rare beauty with dark brown eyes, high cheekbones and hair of dark chestnut. She climbed the side of the base of Calabrian Mountains in the south of Italy on a windy, sunny day with her mother to pick wild fruit on the family farm. They had separated for a while as a pair of anxious eyes was watching from a short distance behind the brambles near a cherry tree. The eyes watched the lithe arm reaching for the fruit and placing most in her apron to be put eventually into a small sack nearby.

The eyes coveted her body and face. They slowly ran up and down from her head to her half-covered shapely calves as she reached for the free bounty of the mountain. The heart of the interloper was beginning to beat within his chest as a blacksmith's anvil being beaten rapidly by a hot hammer. His legs were set apart for balance to spring sideways and reach her in two or three of her heartbeats. His hand perspired as he gripped his knife more firmly.

As he waited anxiously for the older woman to widen the gap in her search, he constantly gauged all the distances among the three, there on the lonely mountain side. Thoughts surely must have raced across his mind, to put away his knife and walk back down the path he used to follow the women. Surely he knew that what he was about to do was a heinous act loathed by God and man. He must have been close to folding the glistening blade, but as do most evil acts, they go forward to fruition with little or no restraint until the great impulse is satiated by flood and screams. So it must have been with Francesco Mattera that blue summer day in the hot glare of August.

The young girl, Alba, started to hum and sing one of her many love songs as she reached for an unusually large purple fig just above her reach. She must have that one and eat it there, savoring i ts delectable meat and grind the small delicate seeds as part of the reward. She placed the fruit from her apron into the sack at her feet toO enhance a longer reach and jump for the prize.

The blade of his knife was sheathed for some unfathomable reason; perhaps it was conscience, perhaps fear of the consequences if he were caught, imprisonment, retribution by her family or perhaps, pity. He was not wholly evil. There were occasions when he helped people courteously, helping older men and women in and out of his livery carriage; lovingly taking care of his horse and giving the poor children of the village free rides when he was going somewhere without a passenger. The thousand good characteristics resided with ten evil ones for the equipoised conflict for his soul, but an evil trait is perhaps one-hundred times the weight of a good one.

The older woman called something to her and the girl answered above the gentle wind. After retrieving the succulent fig and enjoying it as her last, she moved up the incline away from her mother for the last picks of the day. Around a slight bend, she was now completely out of the older woman's sight. Any screams now would be carried by the winds to the valley and dissipated to unhearing ears far below.

Mattera half-circled silently to a new vantage point, hidden like a crawling cat approaching its unsuspecting prey, gauging, watching, checking as his hand again grasped the knife and exposed the steel talon to the golden sunlight. It *would* do its work after all, resulting in blood on the steel. The smaller evils overcame the larger good and thoughts of tolerance, love of humanity and goodness, racing across his mind, were stifled and silenced. God was cast out of his soul that morning on the mountain as his moment had come.

In four silent steps he approached her from the rear and was upon her like a wolf of ancient times on his unaware prey. The iron grasp of his left arm and hand around her neck and mouth was unbreakable by this frightened girl. Her widened eyes recognized him. For a brief moment she thought it was just a bad joke; just a young man jokingly frightening a young girl. Perhaps she thought he played this charade because he really liked her and a romance would blossom from the incident. But this was not the case, for the blade held close to her left jaw moved quickly and sliced open the alabaster flesh studded with many tiny beauty marks.

Although her mouth was slightly uncovered, she did not scream. She felt no pain as the bright crimson fluid ran down in a sticky cascade between his fingers. As he released her, she began to feel the great sting of the wound. He walked away quickly like a cowardly jackal, yelling, "If I can't have you, then no one now will want you - except me!"

In the days that followed, he was arrested by the *carabinieri* and held in jail until he was remanded for trial in the Supreme Court of the Province of Calabria.

Alba's greater wound was spiritual, not being able to understand the disfigurement perpetrated in the name of love.

Mattera had declared his love for her, but her father, a respected architect and published poet, had rejected him as a proper suitor for the hand of one of his daughters. Matters' twisted dementia believed that this was a vehicle to circumvent the edict of my grandfather.

The man was lucky in many ways even without the fulfillment of his desire. He was incarcerated before he could be repaid; her brothers, my uncles, were of such personalities of noblesse oblige who, fortunately for the assailant, believed in the justice of the law; my grandfather allowed him to live; my brother, a Turk. of the highest order, was too young - seven-years-old - to seek justifiable vengeance; and I - I had yet to be born.

Weeks followed and the trial of Francesco Mattera began in the packed courtroom of the Supreme Court. The prisoner was guarded and flanked by two carabinieri, with their dark uniforms and Napoleonic type hats with red plumes. A large crucifix hung on the wall above the three magistrates' heads with a portrait of Victor Emmanuel, the king, above them. Two Italian tricolors of green, white and red adorned both corners of the front of the room whose white walls were composed of sturdy cured lime and sand.

Witnesses were called establishing times, places and events. The families concerned were present, one to see just punishment for a dastard savage and cowardly attack on a helpless girl with a spotless reputation, and the other hoping for blind justice not to hear.

The defendant's widowed mother was in the front row incessantly reciting the Rosary, the simple beads invisible against her black garments. His older brother was sitting next to her holding his farmer's hat in his hands.

All of my family was present except my grandfather. Although he had migrated to Argentina, his prodigious patriarchal presence and influence reached far over the sea and permeated the small courtroom that day. My mother, Alba's older sister, was present, acting as his vicar.

Alba was in the courtroom with her jaw still bandaged from the surgeon's skilled hand. There was no plastic surgery in those days. The sutures were fine and the wound bathed with antiseptic and oil the first few days as it sealed. She wore a bandage under her chin and tied on the top of her head to compress the inner bandage beneath it. The surgeon had a sterile, oil-soaked compress on the skin, hopefully to keep the scar tissue forming to be minimal.

The defense attorney pleaded that although possibly guilty, the defendant was insane with frustrated, unrequited love for this girl. In his twisted logic, he thought that no one would have her if she were disfigured and that he alone would claim her. The counselor asked for mercy from the court.

The King's prosecutor argued that the despicable act cried out for the most punishment allowed under the law. No woman was safe from maiming if this crime's punishment were not severe. The message must be sent that such an action is intolerable in a civilized society. "Animals" like the defendant were not fit to live among decent citizens.

She was called to the stand trembling with anxiety, as the silent spectators held their breaths. Her shyness also played against her. With a subdued voice she told the incident of that day, looking down mostly on her folded hands.

After many questions, she cried silently, mostly out of the fear and shyness innate to her nature.

Mattera looked straight ahead without emotion; there was no discernible remorse in his cold stare forward.

Finally, nearing the end of his summation, the prosecuting attorney, turning partly to the packed courtroom, asked " . . . and because of this disfigurement to this beautiful, innocent girl, who would want this poor girl now?"

My father's nephew, Rudolfo, a young man of twenty, who loved Alba from afar for a year, stood in the middle of the silent sea of shocked faces and announced loudly, "I would!"

Mattera served but a little over a year in an Italian prison and thereafter escaped with his life, however miserable must have been its nature.

Although their life together was not without salt, tragedy and pain, Rudolfo once stated to my sister, many years later in Argentina where they lived, that all he needed out of life was a tent to live in and his Alba of the mountains.

Mattera became the town drunkard.

My paternal cousin and maternal aunt were married for forty-one years. She died in Buenos Aires in 1980.

TOO MANY BRASS RINGS

Rodie ran the merry-go-round on Route 110. He enjoyed watching the children waving, smiling and laughing. The children's parents held them regardless of the thick leather straps securing them to lacquered moving horses, green turtles and miniature giraffes. He relished being close to the blue or deep brown eyes watching his movements as he secured them onto a quiet solid beast. When they sometimes looked up with curiosity at the old man with the gray hair and short white bears, some suspected he had another identify.

He would furtively wink and smile at them, most often not garnering a reaction, let alone a smile. There was still a remnant of the strength of youth, like the crumbling stones of a pyramid.

The park was closing and moving south to more lucrative fields. He owned his concession, not like others who leased or ran them for a large company. This was his last season and he decided not to go south. He'd given the ride to his only relative in the country, a niece in Florida.

At noon, a small school bus full of children and a pleasant looking full figured woman got off and approached the entrance of his ride. She handed him eleven tickets as she greeted him cordially, her hazel eyes and broad smile showed genuine gladness.

"How are you, Mr. Rodie?"

"Fine, fine thank you." His head tilted, not recognizing her.

"Sam . . . Samantha Reyes. I was in your American History class in high school and your neighbor. Remember?"

"Samantha, I'm sorry, I didn't recognize you. How are you?" he asked as she hugged him warmly.

"Fine, and how's Mrs. Rodie?"

"She passed away a year ago."

"Oh, I'm sorry, I didn't know. She was such a kind person," she said.

"Yes, well her passing was a blessing. So you're teaching," he said quickly changing the subject, "and . . . ?"

"And I got married three years ago and have a baby boy. Here's his picture," she said producing a snapshot.

"Handsome little devil," said Rodie. "What's his name?"

"Tommy Lee. I named him after your son because he always treated me so nice even after he graduated."

"Sounds like you had a little crush on him, Sam."

"It was more than 'a little',"

"I'm sorry. We didn't know. Well, let's get your class on these animals, shall we? The turtles need a lot of exercise you know," he chuckled as he smiled.

She introduced him to her class, saying that he was once her teacher. They orchestrated a hello almost in unison.

After strapping each student, limping to each child, the old man started his ride as the animals seemed to come to life with the music and crashing cymbals. The wooden beasts received the instant love of their temporary masters. The children were treated to the longest ride in the park's history. The repertoire of glorious songs and waltzes ran three times, ending with the Blue Danube. Without looking, Rodie declared that a lucky ticket had been turned in for free rides. He put up a 'Closed' sign and asked who wanted a new animal, then rearranging some of the children. He moved the steel rings from the dispensing apparatus and substituted the whole box of a dozen spare brass rings. He slowed the ride to a crawl so that every child could easily grab one. All but one were successful. Then Jennifer's giraffe was stopped next to the ring as she plucked her stationary prize with ease. Tears metamorphasized into a smile as Rodie had her take an extra 'golden' ring.

He then gave them six more cycles. They 'won' all the prizes he had on his shelf which consisted of dolls, hats with fluffy fuchsia feathers and paper-mache canaries on a stick and string which chirped as the tail feathers spun. He refused the brass rings back, having them keep them as 'magic lucky pieces.' Most children thanked him. Samantha had to refuse a seventh magical trip since the bus was scheduled to take them back to school.

As she was loading and checking them on the bus, Rodie asked her to come into his trailer for something he wanted her to have. He opened a military trunk in a corner and removed a carefully wrapped package of letters and placed it in her bare hand, then supported it with his.

"These are from Tommy," he said. "He wrote about how he felt about things in general and the war. I know you'd appreciate them."

At first she refused them as too valuable to him, but he insisted, saying he has memorized them. He was heading south, traveling light, leaving most of his possessions behind. She accepted the letters with deep gratitude. Just having them in her hands, and later to be reading *his* words, would make her heart pound even faster.

"Thank you, but are you sure?"

He nodded as his eyes closed. They walked slowly toward the waiting bus.

"Could you come to dinner this Saturday? I'd like you to meet my husband and little Tommy," she asked.

"Thank you, Samantha. I'd be most pleased, but we're leaving in the morning. I'll be gone before the holidays."

"Tonight then . . . for a simple meal of frankfurters, backed potatoes and a cold Dutch beer. I could whip up that gourmet meal in about six minutes," she pursued.

"I'm expecting a call from Columbia some time tonight. My brother."

"Perhaps when you come back then."

"Yes, perhaps. Thank you."

She kissed him on one cheek as she held the other. Her perfume and soft leather glove reminded him of his wife and of subtle fragrances and gentle spring days. He again mused how perfume enhances a woman's beauty.

She left with the children waving joyful goodbyes to the nice man with the ride of wonderment, beautiful music and magic rings. The school buss pulled away with a roar of smoking fumes.

* * *

As the winter sun set, he put his call through to his brother.

"John, how are you? Merry Christmas," crackled a voice over hundreds of hills and valleys.

"Fine, Billy. Merry Christmas. How are you?"

"Good, good. We're preparing for the Christmas pageant. Why don't you come down? I'd really like to see you, John."

"Who wouldn't? I'd love to, Billy, but . . . I've got packing to do for the winter season. I'm giving the ride to Marcy. After it gets set up in Florida, someone will run it for her."

"Johnny, we can have a few laughs and talk about old times. John . . . John, you still here?"

"Yes . . . "

"Are you all right? Come down, please."

"I'm fine, Billy, fine. I just need a rest. I'm retiring for the second time, you know. I just had a wonderful bunch of school kids on the ride. I think we may have broken the world's record on the number of rides and brass rings they won," he chuckled and finally laughed. "Maybe we'd make it in Guiness'."

"It's good to hear you laugh again, Johnny."

"Don't worry about me, will you? Remember *I'm* the older brother. I'm supposed to worry about you, but you were always a pain in my ass, Father Bill, until you ran off and decided to be a 'nun'," he joked.

"*You* were the pain in the ass. I had to help the big brain in math."

They both laughed heartily, followed by silence.

"Listen, Billy, I've got to go now. Have a nice holiday, OK? I love you, Bill."

"I will. See you soon and I love you too, Johnny. Take good care of yourself."

After the click and buzz, he set the phone down slowly.

Rodie went to his tape player and inserted his specially made tape of his wife's favorite pieces and songs, starting with the resounding "March of the Siamese Children" and ending with "Swan Lake."

He could play it loud since he was away from the other trailers; the park was closing and most of the proprietors had left.

Gyrene Morton popped his head in and asked, "Captain, you comin' with us for a holiday drink before we pull stakes in the morning?"

"Maybe later, Gyrene. I've got a slight headache. But come on in. We'll have one last drink of good stuff, in case I can't make it."

He opened his cupboard and took out a half-full quart of Chivas Regal and tumblers. He filled them and drank his with slow ease while his friend gulped it down like a goldfish on a campus. They spoke of the trip to Florida and fishing. They discussed things like the end of the war, great battles of Europe and the South Pacific, and Hitler's mistakes. They ended with horrors about which neither had ever spoken: one describing the walking, crying skeletons of Buchenwald; the other of finding his two missing buddies in an Iwo Jima cave hanging dead by their ankles, skinned alive. The invisible bond between them solidified more.

"When are ya gonna be there, Cap'n?" asked Morton finally as he rose. "The girls will be there too. Evelyn'll ask for you."

"Don't wait for me if you decide to go any place else. I can always find you."

"OK, Cap'n," said the tall gray man as he stepped down from the trailer.

"Gyrene . . . "

"Yeah, Cap'n."

"My first name is John."

"I know that, sir."

"What's yours?"

After hesitating, he said, "Morton, Augustus C., Sgt. USMC 237209, sir."

"Merry Christmas, Gus."

"Merry Christmas, sir."

* * *

His eyes no longer teared as the fluid lava scorched its way down and burst in his stomach. He gazed at a family picture of his smiling blonde wife and their small son on her lap. They were sitting in a swing set . . . an eon ago.

As the finale of "Man of LaMancha" rumbled gloriously to a conclusion, he sang a few lines as he had always done.

I am I, Don Quixote, the Lord of LaMancha and . . . (stumbling on the words) . . . to destiny I go. And the wild winds of fortune will carry me onwards to withersoever they blow, withersoever they blow, onward to glory I go!"

He sipped another tumbler slowly to emptiness.

A rendition of Como's "Wind Beneath My Wings" started. His wife would always chime in with the lyrics: "Did you ever know that you're my hero?"

He'd interpose on occasion, "Did you ever know that I'm your hero?" Launching her giggling, then ending the song together.

He was up again to the cupboard for his last bottle of Jack Daniels, Black Label. He was not yet drunk, but the alcohol permeated his brain dulling the sharp crystals of unwanted memories.

He limped to his military locker box, knelt on his good knee and dug past the dark khaki blouse and light trousers neatly folded and encased in clear plastic. He pushed past his barracks cap with the tarnished brass eagle, his officer's hardware, the Purple Heart and combat ribbons, down deep to the left of the trunk. There was a hefty object wrapped in oil cloth. He brought the object to the table where he meticulously wiped it clean between sips.

The last selection started, a double entry of "Swan Lake," his wife's favorite. He consumed his final glass, feeling the welcomed numbing glow. The exalting strains of the music lifted his spirit to painless heights, past long dark tunnels of memory and finally into bittersweet reverie.

He looked deep into his wife's eyes and warm smile, his young son's fixed laughing countenance, then to the other photograph of his son squatting in camouflage fatigues wearing a coolie straw and bamboo hat, holding an automatic rifle by one hand and a small shy-looking oriental boy on his knee.

Tom was killed two weeks after this photograph was taken.

The last drink went untouched until a stranger's hands threw it away . . . before the trailer went south.

COLUMBUS BEAT ME HERE

Columbus beat me here by four hundred and forty-four years. One of the many other major differences between us is that I landed in Brooklyn as my final destination. He planted a banner on the beach of San Salvador, carried all the way from Spain. I wanted to plant a wooden hobby horse on the floor of our new home, a cold water railroad flat in Bay Ridge. We brought it all the way from Naples. I missed the horse instantly as I stepped onto the wooden ramp of the pier, meeting my father for the very first time. He was already an American citizen when we arrived. It was either mugged or stolen or my father threw it away. I was told many years later, he intended to buy me a new one after he met us at the pier in Manhattan. As we got off the ship, the Vulcania, I asked about it as we walked toward my cousin, Johnny's, cab. My father laughed, telling me it swam back to Italy. Being a four-year-old mental midget, I believed him. He never saw me before, or I him, so I had every reason to trust him. That horse, as an antique today, would probably be worth a few thousand dollars. But regardless of the value, I wanted, and to this day sixty years later, I still want that freaking horse!

I never asked about it until I was fifty-years-old, constantly seeing it in a picture with my hand resting on it like Hop-a-long Cassidy holding his placid beast. That old man screwed me out of my horse! Now that I think of it, it was asinine to bring the horse with us three thousand miles and then letting it free.

There was little I remember before I arrived. I remember falling into a black marbled kitchen sink, where I was given my baths. I hit my head against it once, but forgot the pain. I remember rubbing the wings of a huge butterfly hidden behind a portico door on a balcony facing the Mediterranean. My 'crazy' older brother, Emilio, placed it there for some reason. The wings were slippery and powdery. He was always catching birds in the nearby woods, applying a heavy gooey mucilage to the top of branches where he knew they would perch. The next day he would climb up to the branch and remove the unlucky animal with the ease of a great hunter. He would sell most of them for food to the local gentry. He kept a few in cages after blinding them with a red-hot wire by barely touching the eyes, as Samson was blinded by the Philistines. When I asked him why would one perform such a savage and incomprehensible act, he explained with a hunter's logical certitude and acumen, that it was the way to make the canary-like birds great singers, since then they had nothing else better to do.

He was well known in the small town of San Lucido, one hundred and twenty miles south of Naples as a young 'turk', who respected no custom, obeyed no rules, and gave no obeisance to clergy. To this day, he is probably still remembered by the survivors of the area. Once, as a ten-year-old, he passed a young village priest without acknowledgments and received the stroke of a small staff across the back of his legs.

When, with indignant anger, he defiantly asked why he had been assaulted, the priest explained it was to teach him manners and respect in greeting his ecclesiastical superiors. The unfortunate vain priest was pelted unmercifully for an hour with hard-thrown stones from a safe distance. On occasion, the father would try to catch him, but that was impossible due to my brother's fleetness and the drag factor of the priest's cassock. I don't mean to say he was in drag, at least at that time of the day. Eventually, he was, like a defeated crusader, forced to retreat shouting, *bestio, filgio d' putana*. To this day, I hypothesize that if the priest is still alive and living in the town, he has my brother's picture, frontal and side view on his wall in the vestry with a posted reward under it.

When he complained to our mother who was considered a respected matriarchal Calpurnia whose father was an architectural engineer and published poet, about her son's abominable actions, she asked him a simple question which reduced him and his anger to a minuscule squeaking Liliputian. The question was, "Did you call my son 'the won of a whore'?"

Recently, I offered the *turk* a Certificate of Indulgence signed by Pope John the 23rd. It was given me as a token of appreciation for refusing payment in tutoring the nephew of an archbishop. I was willing to sign it over to my brother as one would sign over a stock or a bond. It supposedly insures that I would not have to spend any time in Purgatory, presuming I am on my way to heaven. I presume that I am and I don't expect any blaring bugles or drum rolls, but I plan to make it, even if I have to sneak in under the pearly gates. Now that I am getting on in years, I took the precaution to have the Certificate protected by laminated asbestos, just in case of a house fire.

Anyway, *Turko* told me to shove it up where the sun don't shine. He doesn't need it! If he doesn't need it, then nobody does.

Another fond memory of Italy was walking to town about a mile away, as a four-year-old wearing potato sack-like garments. I bought an ice called *gellato*. It was the most delicious taste of an icy dessert I had ever tasted, still to this day. Now that I'm retired, I may go back to Italy to recapture the delectability of that lost taste. It would only cost me a presumptive $5,000.

On the way back home, I remember going past the garbage dump and looking down the steep incline of debris. There was a dead black and white dog at the bottom, which I thought of bringing home. I thought better of it because Calpurnia allowed no pets in the house.

The multicolored pebbles on the beach of the Mediterranean were beautiful as the clear azure waves lapped gently against it. One could clearly see two or three fathoms down to the rocky green bottom through the fantastically lucid clear water. The sun shone with its hot glaring brilliance like a beneficent furnace in the blue sky. My brother took me out in a row boat and I looked down at the waving kelp and dark round stones. There were sea urchins to be found there which were eaten with gusto as a delicacy after the removal of the tops like a marine Jack-O-Lantern. The delicious odor of the clean brine emanated from the dipped bread of the echinoderm's interior. I wonder if they're still delectable with the pollution of the water from distant Yugoslavian factories.

My sister used to take me to the beach down a small stone retaining wall. We picked prickly pears and ate them. We had to cross a small farm where two other children lived that we were friendly with but not too friendly. Their father had a bullwhip on his belt on most occasions, so we just kept walking to the beach to swim.

My sister, Aldesia, loved the sea. She often would foolishly swim out too far, not thinking or knowing of an undertow and currents.

My last major memory was that of sitting outdoors on a starry night. A huge screen showing a black and white movie could be seen in the dark distance. It was a magical thing to see, gigantic black and white figures and faces talking. It could have been *It Happened One Night* or a propaganda film on Mussolini. Who knows? I could not understand it, nor did I care. It was just magic.

I don't remember leaving the limestone house facing the sea with the marble stairs to the second floor, nor the huge black iron cross on the road into town. I don't remember the train ride to Naples as the embarkation point.

I DO remember part of the trip across the Atlantic, because my mother threatened to throw me overboard. For some unknown reason, I would cry and moan for hours at a time. I was taken and checked by the ship's doctor who could find no physiological problems. However, the incessant crying continued until Calpurnia could stand it no more and stuck my head out a porthole and threatened to throw me into the Atlantic far, far below. My crying stopped instantly. My sister could now return to the peace and quiet of the stateroom, while my brother was out having fun, roaming the decks hunting the ship for priests.

We must have passed the Statue of Liberty on that September day in 1936, for we landed at a Manhattan pier, but I have no recollection of the beautiful green lady of the harbor. I would see her continually growing up in Brooklyn from the hills of Sunset Park. She was exceptionally beautiful at night in the harbor - like a great beacon that she is. The green copper sulfates and oxide of her make up led me to believe that she was part of the Emerald City that I and millions of others saw in the Wizard of Oz a few years later.

Traveling from the pier in Manhattan across the Brooklyn Bridge was a trip no less enthralling than one on the star ship Enterprise as the sun went down in the western orange and flame skies. We drove through downtown Brooklyn to Fifth Avenue past my father's little shoe repair shop on 46th Street but continued on to 51st. There were pink, red and glowing neon lights from the bars, penny arcade and flashing running white lights from movie marquises and furniture stores. It was the land of Oz. I had only seen lights and objects in black and white at night, colored lights, neon lights were miracles of science.

We continued on to Bay Ridge Avenue and turned left up to 11th Avenue and stopped the magic machine that moved without horses. We had arrived at my great aunt's house to stay for a few days until my father set up a railroad apartment on 47th Street and Fifth Avenue near his shop.

Unknown to me at the time, my Great-Aunt Amelia was my mother's aunt. Like most children, I didn't know the specific relationships in a family. Some people are called uncle or aunt without being true relatives so they can address the adults by name rather than Mr. or Mrs.

As we entered the green glass enclosed porch (again Emerald City) and into the comfortable, modestly furnished living room, we were introduced to the rest of the strangers of the amiable family. I met my third cousin, Stephen, known as Skippy. I could speak no English, and he spoke no Italian. When he spoke, it sounded like gibberish as I had not heard a different language until that day. I asked my mother what was wrong with his tongue. Was it broken and he couldn't speak proper Italian or what?

I could speak very well and could recite some poetry, whose or what I don't remember, but I was asked to recite some that evening, probably to the dismay of my linguistically disabled cousin. In my gratitude for the applause and the dinner prepared that evening, I felt an obligation to do something beneficent for my new found family. For whatever reason, even to this day escapes me, I warned my aunt not to leave her pocketbook out during the night as a precaution against theft. Well, that made the crap hit the fan the next day at the breakfast table when Calpurnia found out about my statement. Had there been a high porthole in the room, I think I would have been shot out without warning or hesitation, reciting poetry or not.

In the days we were there, Skippy showed me the fun of running up and down the high dirt mounds across the street where they were constructing new homes. These were as steep as the hill at the dump but much more fun. There were no dead dogs to trip over as you reached bottom. I don't remember how we communicated, but we must have, either by a few words or by sign language. We visited his mother and father who lived a few houses down the street in a large house. His mother, Urselia, was my mother's cousin. She was a very amiable pleasant woman but was emaciated with the ravages of tuberculosis and too sickly to have come over the first day of our stay. Years later, after the war, she would pass away after living a few years in the Catskills where her husband, Steve, took her in a valiant but a vain attempt to cure her of the disease.

When our apartment was ready, we moved into our mansion nicely decorated with prime oak furniture, fresh from the Salvation Army on Third Avenue. The dining room mirror had three sections of carved and frosted glass on the edges. The kitchen in the rear looked out to the rear yard which we had no access to because we were on the second floor above Hansen Brothers' store which was a huge well-maintained music and record store that also sold shinny brass musical instruments and drums. There was a pleasant saleslady there who walked, it seemed, mostly on her toes gliding back and forth between the counter and the rest of the large store. In the years to come, I would name her in my mind 'Twinkletoes' as she flitted along Fifth Avenue with a pasted half smile on her face. As I write this now about this pleasant, mysterious woman, I am saddened to realize that if she had no surviving relatives. I noticed throughout the years, I noticed she had no wedding band on her hand when I would go into the store to buy records. This would be the only evidence of her existence; that she passed through this life as a lady walking with that permanent smile on her face.

We didn't stay in that apartment too long because my father found another apartment directly across the street from his shop for five dollars a month less. By today's standards, it is a pittance, but in those days it was more than a week's wages to an average working person. To my father, it must have been an excellent move to save that week's wages and be able to have more food on the table for the month. It turned out, like most things in life, less than moderately beneficial, having the good and the bad, the ying and the yang, the sweet and the bitter come together in an indissoluble marriage. Things would later develop slowly or explode onto the scene in the slow motion passage of time.

One of the 'yangs' we had to endure for this new ying of saving five dollars, was that, as we slept in one of the rear bedrooms, my sister and I were awakened by scratching noises near the windows facing Fifth Avenue. Against the pinkish glare of the magical pink neon and street lights, we saw the source of the noise. Two dark animals were climbing up the curtains of one of the windows, for what purpose, to this day I cannot imagine. Somehow I knew that it was not right to have these rodents living in the house with us, regardless of whether they were paying rent or not. I thought at the time they must have belonged in Sunset Park with the others living in the trees there. The park rodents were much cuter with their bushy tails; these were darker and had bald tails being two large rats. Perhaps through my sister's fear, I sensed they should not be in the rooms, so I picked up a shoe near the side of the bed and threw it at them, just barely missing the window. Thank God for that, for it would have blown my father's five dollar savings for the month and they retired for the night.

A strange land, this America, where ugly squirrels lived in the same house instead of goats and pigs as I saw in the little farm house below us.

* * *

In November of 1936, I saw the miracle of snow for the first time in my life. It was so clean and white as it lay on the glass milk bottle outside the kitchen window. I decided to taste it. It wasn't particularly tasty, but it was cold. How unfortunate God did not decide to manufacture the manna with a touch of lemon and sugar with the gallato in San Lucido. Nevertheless, I continued to eat it to my fill. I opened the round cardboard top of the milk bottles on the fire-escape which was in the process of freezing and drank the half cup of cold thick cream floating at the top. The rusty black fire-escape was transformed into an artwork covered in part with the pristine flakes of snow.

When I went outside to play in the stuff, dressed warmly in knickers, long socks, shoes, (we didn't know what galoshes were) and my warm hat that looked like a World War I pilot's hat, buckled tightly under my chin, I braved the cold for as long as I could with wet socks and shoes - ten minutes. When I came in and changed to the warmth and smell of the kitchen cooking, I was the richest boy on earth, especially when my mother handed me a cooked sausage on a fork right out of the percolating tomato sauce of the Sunday meal. Chunks of pork and fat steamed after the first nibble. There were delectable grains of fennel seed waiting to tantalize the palate after breaking them. They burst forth their sweet flavor like blasts of fireworks at Coney Island on summer Tuesday nights.

But then, another miracle and reward, for which I did not know the reason, my mother, no longer the ogre threatening to cast me into the Atlantic, resupplied my fork with a masterpiece of culinary art, a meatball. It has been sixty years from that day and I have not been able to recapture the delectability of the exact taste of both tidbits. They are probably lost forever in the sausage maker's formula and Calpurnia's mixing ingredients in the culinary crucibles.

My sister and brother were, of course, jealous of the brat who should have been sacrificed to Neptune as an offering for safe passage, for the exodus, and the sanctity of silence. They almost had their chance. If they could have bumped my mother's arms to relinquish her grasp as I was being held halfway out of the porthole, it would have looked like an accident, but they lost it. The time and opportunity of kismet opening the door to opportunity were for the briefest of moments as a sad consequence for them. They had to suffer my presence on this planet for the next sixty years.

As the first summer came to a close and school began in September in the Kindergarten of Public School No. 2, we danced to the sound of piano played in staccato, drew pictures in crayon and drank warm milk from a small wax container, the golden doors to America and a lifetime had widely swung open for me.

What was to follow was an almost normal life in this magical land of pink and green neon lights. This was to be a land of paradoxes and ironies drawn from honey, silk and steel. This wonderful Land of Oz.

DANDELIONS FOR IVAN PETROV

Petrov's horse had a shattered right rear leg caused by French grapeshot and tumbled forward in a complete somersault on the slippery, grassy incline. It landed on her master's torso and got up wild-eyed and in excruciating pain. The right rear leg was mangled and hanging by shredded tendons as it hobbled away on three legs, then stumbled to earth for the last time. It was shot a half-hour later by a passing Russian Infantryman who loved horses. The soldier in the red cassock uniform merely glanced in Petrov's direction and continued walking while reloading his musket. He was advancing onto the field of exploding Napoleonic cannons on the ridge ahead. The artillery spilling blue-gray smoke and death seemed ineffectual at that moment in time on the green battlefield.

Petrov's right rib cage was shattered; two ribs punctured his lung severely in five places a chunk of metal had gone through one shoulder, just missing the heart, but both wounds were lethal. He would be dead by the time the bugles sounded to retire for the night. It would not be an easy death for this Russian farmer. His only consolation was that he would not be alone in his suffering. His brother and best friend, would find him at the end of the battle where both French and Russians searched the field for fallen comrades, mostly ignoring, but sometimes greeting each other with sad eyes.

His brother, Illiah, and cousin, Pietre, found him and carried him on a makeshift stretcher made of muskets and bloody tunics of the dead. He was laid by a glowing campfire near a small tent and was tended to frantically by the two men. The labored breathing and gurgling sounds coming from his throat were harbingers of the peace that was to come.

The rumor spreading like horizontal sheet lightning through the many camps was that a permanent truce had been declared. It became reality after a fortnight of rumors. It *had* been the last battle. Tomorrow, the French would begin their withdrawal from the harsh Russian land, even though they had spent the winter in Moscow with little food and supplies. The Russians had laid waste to their own land in the path of the voracious Napoleon. The Russian winter and Siberian winds off the icy tundra had caused the defeat of the invaders as would have ten thousand more spewing cannons.

Ivan's lung had ceased its flow of blood during the long evening to a trickle, but the other wound was too massive for self repair. Illiah had brought the regimental doctor to the tent after begging him with tears in his eyes, to look at his brother. Pietre would have brought him at a sword point, for they were not only cousins, but the best of friends.

The bearded doctor examined his wounds with close scrutiny and shook his head as he looked into the others' eyes.

"Make him as comfortable as you can," he said simply.

Just before midnight, the unconscious Ivan passed into memory where he would live for a lifetime. At dawn's weak light, they buried him in a grave with a cross made from his broken saber and a wooden crossbar bearing his name and age of nineteen.

Days l ater, as the army was disbanding, they approached the top of the ridge mound where he rested among the hundreds of other dead. The horses grazed the top of the hill as Illiah knelt. He swore to himself that he'd never let his mother know of his brother's death. She was in the dark, twilight of her years and knowing of his death would only quicken her own.

He would invent a story of his brother being chosen by the General's staff as a gallant cavalryman to travel as protector of a small commission to France to supplement the peace treaty. He would write to his illiterate mother and read the letters "from France" for years to come. He would forego his trip to the university until his mother passed away, reading to her every month, letters of love and obeisance from his younger brother. His plans and goals had crumbled before the cannon, smoke and blood of the field.

The spring morning found the withdrawal of the long moving queue of silent beaten French snaking west along the semi-muddy roads. Illiah and Pietre rode up to the ridge where Ivan's grave rested among hundreds of fallen heroes whose only heroic act was being on the field filled with apprehension and awe before being struck down by fate or chance.

The green field of the recently rent earth of cannon ball and spade was expansive under the blue morning sky. Departing comrades were interspersed in the field of the fallen. Along side Ivan's plot was a woman tending her son's grave, kneeling, arranging small stones and removing remnant weeds from the clumps of earth coldly blanketing her son's body. She made a simple bower of bright yellow dandelions to place at the head of the grave. An older man stood above her in silence, holding his peasant's hat needlessly by both hands. Her squarish countenance was the force of Mother Russia. It already had been browned in the cold spring's sun and wind, working the fields.

The men were ready to depart and join the massive queue below in the valley heading home. Albeit the armies were moving in opposite directions. There was a hope, a dream for all, a thought coruscating in every brain, swelling in every chest. Regardless of the color of the uniform that thought, that idea was the ultimate grand reward for all soldiers, the vanquished as well as the victors . . . home, home.

He took a small stone from his brother's grave and carefully placed it in his tunic. As he stood up to mount, the woman cleaved her golden bower of dandelions and handed half to him with glistening eyes. He slowly took them and placed them at the head of the grave, then gently cupped her sun browned cheek in his hand for but a moment and mounted to slowly join the movement and disharmony below.

FATHER 'THUNDERBIRD JACK'

C-10 is an island prison in the temperate zone of the Lesser Antilles, north of South America. It is inhabited predominantly by convicted murderers in the second degree, some with their families who have voluntarily chosen to come with them. There are no guards or containing walls per se. They are free to live independently or on one of the five existing communes. Heads of accompanying families are issued advanced laser-directed automatic shotguns which fire from the initial wide spread for self-defense to a closed pattern of a meter. Single women convicts are issued standard shotguns.

Of the five, mostly agrarian communes, only one is strictly for 'outmates' with families. The rest are optional. There are communes with mostly homosexuals, one predominantly black with or without families, one for single outmates and one non-agrarian, hunting societies who raid their neighbors and hunt for game, animals and fellow humans. They are the Hunter Clan.

Twice a month, the communes gather to trade at the Hub, a circular open area whose borders are contiguous to the five communes. Mainland merchants, protected by the island militia, are allowed to trade also. They purchase a franchise for two hundred thousand North American units. In the year 2107, the United States, Canada and Mexico, merged by tripartite referendum into the New United States of North America.

The island is unsupervised, the 'outmates' must fend and protect themselves. At the end of the day, the merchants and soldiers retreat to the military compound on the southern tip of the island and lock the prisoners out.

From the "Number Five" commune, an inter-racially mixed family, with their friends, eased out of the ox-drawn carts. This commune, like most, allowed single and married prisoners who have their families with them. Another such commune allowed only families. One commune was distinctive because there were few families per se, due to the heavy gravitation of homosexual and lesbian prisoners, but they did not discriminate. If straight convicts opted to live there due to the minimal violence and killings of all the five communes, they were welcomed.

The mixed family from Five was made up of J. J. Cutherford, a white man of 32. He stood 5' 11" and his African American paramour, Helen Pernell and her two children, Jason, 12, and Diamond Champagne, 9. She was a full-figured six feet tall beauty with short cropped hair and gold earrings bouncing occasionally back from her high, smooth, chocolate colored cheekbones. She wore a denim skirt and vest and soft leatherette, rough-surfaced light brown boots laced just below her knees. They were open on the sides and held in place by leather thongs which criss-crossed to below her knee.

The couple had met when Cutherford, while hunting the hills, had come upon a clearing near a promontory where they habituated in a well-concealed nearby cave. Helen had been stunned and tied by the wrists to a sapling. She was to be raped by three men who were about to rape her daughter first and another about to cut her son's throat. The small group was lead by an aggressive female-chieftain of the Hunter group, who were not much agrarian, but were hunters, marauders, raiders, pillagers and cannibals.

Cutherford had once witnessed, with friends, a horrific scene of an independent farm family being raped and brutalized by the men and women of a large raiding party. The mail chieftain and other hunters were sodomizing a young boy. Later, he was butchered and devoured.

Luckily for Helen and her children, it had been a small raiding party, for Cutherford quickly, with surprise, dispatched two Hunters and held the others at bay with his weapon, a hunting bow. He held them off until he could recapture Helen's advanced weapon from the female chieftain who laid it down to build a roasting fire. As he vanquished the survivors, Helen attacked the chieftain and broke her nose with repeated punches as she lay on the ground until he stopped it.

A week later, on his return to the cave, he convinced Helen and the children to live with him at his commune, for they were no longer safe at their cave. She explained she was about to leave the island since she had come with a convict who abused her and was about to sexually abuse her daughter. She stole his advanced weapon and hit for a few weeks in a cave near the promontory until she could safely travel to the military compound. There she would ask for asylum and then on the next prison ship to return to the mainland. Now she decided to stay with Cutherford.

In the ensuing months, all went well for the new family unit in the commune, with friends helping to build them a new hut. They had found happiness and love on this Island of Almas Perdidas, as a young Latino prisoner once called it before he committed suicide - an Island of Lost Souls. Albeit a new one was going to be born in the forthcoming months, for Helen and the ecstatic J.J. were going to be parents.

They, along with friends, planned to spend a long weekend at the previous cave abode on a high promontory, camping, swimming, and fishing on the pristine beach below. It was the long four-day holiday which was the 4th of July 2136. The group designed and made a small lightweight sled with wheels pulled by eight dogs. J.J. wanted her trip along the beach to the promontory to be exertion-free, for the one thing he coveted but lacked in his life were children of his own.

They left early Friday afternoon, with friends and children, traveling the safe route with a sailed raft; J.J. and Helen by sled to the adjoining friendly homosexual commune, the Gray Hills Farm. It was decided that while there, a physical with the only obstetrician on the island would be a good idea. J.J. wanted to be certain that all was well for his new son or daughter.

The sled had three steel axles from baby carriages, two under the main seat, and one more in front to support the fulcrum. The six wheels had four inch flat surface areas so they would not dig into the soft earth and the wet sand of the beach on route to the cave, even with the one-hundred-seventy pound Helen sitting in it. It was successfully tested two days before the trip at the shore near the contiguous border of the communes.

J.J. and Helen would follow the first contingent immediately following the early appointment with the obstetrician. They would head northwest to the beach, then travel south to the promontory. A long overall distance, but shorter in travel time. Above all, it was less likely they would meet a hunting party of marauders; if so, the ocean would be a means of escape as it once had served Cutherford.

J.J. estimated to be arriving at the campsite as the coterie was setting up the inflatable tents and the campfires were ablaze at seven-thirty that evening as the sun was setting.

The dogs requisitioned from the commune kennel were in excellent fitness for hauling, of good temperament and properly inoculated. The seventy-six-pound leader, Conan, was powerfully built and obedient. The kennel provided sealed dry rations, a whip for snapping only - no abuse was permitted - and defense. J.J. had a standard greased shotgun in a sealed waterproof container strapped on the side of the sled with the butt slanting diagonally upward in easy reach of the standing driver riding the rear.

The trip began as scheduled. Cutherford did not have to travel to the center of the island, the neutral Hub, where all borders of the territories met. Instead, he used a cleared, well-traveled path which ran laterally to their friendly neighbor's border with whom they were on good terms and did much trading with them. They paused at the fringe and waved to two homosexual guards in the tower. The woman waved them through after stating their business with the obstetrician at the medical hut. The male guard pointed in the same direction they were traveling, but they were told to bear left at the fork a half-mile ahead.

The dogs were easy to handle due to Conan's leadership; they trotted with east at the leisurely 10 miles per hour pace. Cutherford paused for a five minute rest nevertheless and allowed a small drink from a bowl he held for each of the dogs. He petted each saying, "Good boy, Rocky," or "Good girl, Kita," as their name tags showed around their metal collars. They recognized instantly he was a good master with a kind voice and soft hand.

Passing the vast fruit orchards of green oranges, lemons and limes, cornfields and vineyards, they came upon the center of the commune where there was a group of main huts, one of which had a sign made of white birch branches attached to the front wall which read "Council Hall."

J.J. stopped and tied the harness to a porch support. He popped his blonde head in the door and asked, "Pardon me, gentlemen, could you direct me to the medical hut? I've an appointment with Dr. Harrison in a few minutes."

"Are you giving birth soon, honey?" one asked. They all laughed and chuckled.

J.J. smiled along with them, saying, "No, I don't think so, but my woman is."

"Oh, you're the fellow I saw a few months ago," said the same person, "at the Orientation Center. Remember me? I'm Thunderbird Jack."

"Yes, how are you?"

"Fine, thank you. But, you've been a busy little bee, haven't you?"

J.J. didn't respond, but just smiled.

"I heard you hurt one of my jealous bisexual friends in a fight at your farm *over me!*"

"Yes, I'm sorry. I didn't want to hurt him, but he gave me no choice."

"I know, he was such a jealous dick, don't you agree? Just because I made eyes at you that first day, honey. But that's OK, I broke off with him. We don't see each other anymore. He's too jealous, but you might have cured him somewhat. I was hoping you were fighting for my hand in marriage when I heard about it," he joked as the group laughed again.

"No, I'm sorry."

"What a shame, but anyway, I've got me a new girlfriend, Sidney, and she's right over there waving. She's not jealous at all. We understand each other and have an open marriage."

Sidney looked like a two-hundred and thirty pound linebacker in the international football league.

"What's your name, Sweetie?"

"J.J. Cutherford."

"Well, J.J., the hut is just down the road. I'll be glad to show you. I was going there later myself." His four mate friends jeered at the statement.

"I *was*, tell them Sid!" he grinned.

Sidney smiled and made a motion with his right hand as if he was being masturbated.

"Come on, J.J., don't pay any attention to these female apes. They're just jealous because you won my fair hand in combat."

Even J.J. was laughing at that one.

Outside, Cutherford introduced him to Helen and Jack became the perfect cavalier, kissing her hand and saying, "Now I understand why I can't win your heart, J.J. This brown Amazon is too beautiful for words. I hope you don't mind, my dear, if I still keep trying. He's beautiful, too."

J.J. blushed slightly as he guffawed.

"You can try," she said, "I think you might still have a chance."

They all laughed as they liked each other in an instant.

"The hut is around the corner, J.J. It's the third on the left. I'll follow you in a minute. I have to use the 'Ladies Room'."

After securing the dogs in the shade, they entered the hut. The doctor was already there and the examination began immediately, so J.J. stepped outside and saw Jack approaching. Jack offered him a rolled cigarette, but J.J. refused, thanking him and stating that he only smoked cigars. Jack pulled out a cigar from the other pocket of the camouflaged jungle shirt. J.J. graciously accepted, although he quite them months before as a requirement to survive his twenty-year sentence and live out man's longevity of ninety-two years.

"Your woman is truly lovely, J.J. and I *almost* might consider being a heterosexual again. You must have met her on the island. You seemed alone, when you landed months ago."

"Yes, I was. I felt especially alone."

"I know what you mean. But not for too long as it seems she's pregnant. Harrison, by the way, is an excellent doctor. You're very wise in having him check her. You must love her very much."

"I do. I want to marry her before our baby is born. I have to find someone on the island to marry us. Do you know of someone, Jack?"

"You don't need anyone. You can just exchange vows in the absence of a clergyman. That's church policy. But, yes, I know someone who can perform the ceremony. Of what faith are you, if any, not that it matters much here."

"I am a bad Catholic and I think she is also. I mean, she's a

Catholic, since she went to a Catholic high school for a year before she was thrown out. But to tell you the truth, I'm not absolutely sure."

"What did she do, throw a lesbian nun out a window or something?" he joked, "but, anyhow, I can perform the wedding if you wish. Yes, I'm a priest," he continued after seeing the look of disbelief on Cutherford's face. "A defrocked priest, but still always a priest. We have ministers, too. Sidney is a minister. However, there are no rabbis or Muslim clergy as far as I know. They don't get caught as easily as Christians, I surmise."

J.J. was absolutely speechless.

"What's the matter, J.J.? Pussy's got your tongue? Yes, come to think of it, that's probably a very true statement by the looks of that black beauty you have in there. You must feel like old 'Green Horney', or should I say 'The Green Horny." J.J., Sweetie, close your mouth, it's affecting me in the worst way. You know, priests are human too. We make mistakes and sin just like lay people. Please close your mouth before an insect flies in there. Well, do you want me to
perform the ceremony or not?"

"Yes . . . yes, but, but . . . "

"You sound like one of those ancient motor boats, sweetheart. But what, handsome?"

"She's divorced and her husband might still be alive."

"Doesn't matter here. I'm the Archbishop of C-10, self-appointed and self-anointed. I hereby declare her first marriage annulled. Anything else?"

"No, Father Thunderbird," he replied as his shoulder jumped once.

"You know, I'm called that because after the church kicked me out on my sore ass for the extracurricular activities of the 'laying on of two many hands' so to speak, I lived the 'Gay Blade's' life. I drove around each year in the newest Electro-Thunderbird. I can't really blame the Church though, I should not have become a priest after I got out of the army. I had ambivalent feelings which I thought I could control, but I eventually lost out to the 'good life'."

"When did you serve in the army, Jack? I was in the army also."

"Fourteen years ago. I was a Master Sergeant and got out a year after the African War ended. After college, I entered the priesthood."

Helen came out of the hut and smiled at Jack and announced that Dr. Harrison said everything was fine.

"Helen, let me reintroduce you. This gentleman is . . . What's your surname, Jack?"

"Curry."

"Helen Ginger Pernell, I'd like you to meet our very good friend, Father 'Thunderbird' Jack Curry, a Roman Catholic priest and Archbishop of C-10. I want him to marry us, if you would please consent to be my wife."

Helen's mouth opened in utter surprise and after a while she embraced Cutherford tightly, kissed him on the lips and nearly picked him up.

"He's also rescinded your first marriage as Archbishop of C-10."

"Annulled," Jack corrected.

"Annulled."

"Where and when do you want the ceremony. Here or at your farm?" he asked officiously.

After looking at each other for input, Helen said, "At our place in . . . "

"Two weeks," interjected J.J. "We're going to have to make preparations for a very large wedding feast."

"May I bring my girlfriend, Sidney?" asked Jack. "You met him in the Council Hut."

"Certainly, Father, and bring as many friends as you wish. Bring Dr. Harrison also, if you can and he can recheck Helen. It will be a big feast. About how many would you be bringing so we know how much to prepare," he said enthusiastically.

"Would thirty be too many? They won't cause any trouble or commotion."

"Bring forty, if you wish, Father 'T' and thank you very much."

"How about a celebration drink in my hut? I have the best absinthe and green chartreuse smuggled in from France."

"Thank you, Father, but we have to leave right now to meet our friends and children at a preplanned picnic in three hours.

We've got to go the long beach route if we want to make it before dark. But we'll take a raincheck," J.J. told him.

"You got it, kids! In fact, I'll bring so much chartreuse and absinthe to your wedding as a gift, it would float the new Pope's throne. The green chartreuse will straighten out the pubic hairs, believe me! Sometimes, it makes me feel like joining the army again, if I could. Then when I got out the second time, there would be more of us than of you."

"So long, Father. See you in two weeks at our place," said Cutherford.

"Bye, Father. Really glad to meet you," Helen said as she entered the sled and strapped herself in. Jack held out his hand, silently asking for hers again, bowed and kissed it.

"Ciou bambini, vaya con dios," he said. "I've got to brush upon my Latin, you know."

They grinned broadly as J.J. firmly shook hands with him.

"Oh, and J.J., you too, Helen, I want to hear your confessions before the ceremony, and spice them up a bit, will you?" he joked.

"Believe me, Father, we don't have to and as far as Helen is concerned, you'd better bring along your lunch and chartreuse."

Helen slapped his hand on the rail before he could pull it away.

'T' fired off his staccato laughter again. He hadn't laughed like this since his army days.

J.J. snapped the whip high and to the right of Conan's head and urged him onto that steady pace again saying, "Come on, Conan, mush, boy! Better watch those snowbanks!"

Father Thunderbird was now doubled over in laughter, as he tried to wave goodbye, but couldn't. He really liked those people. He resolved to give them the greatest ceremony he ever performed and this time he'd be sober. There would be ample time to float his eyeballs in green chartreuse after the ceremony. He was going all the way. He'd find a black jacket and cut out a simulated white plastic Roman collar from a case of green chartreuse.

He fantasized that the new Pope, Efisio the First, would be proud of him when he heard about it and welcome him back into the fold.

After he saw J.J. and Helen drop out of sight over the hill leading to the beach, he thought it over again, shook his head and said, "Nah."

But, this was going to be *some* 'blowout' or should he say 'feast'!

Father Of Thunderbird Jack

THE KING OF FIELD EXPEDIENCY

Peter Lentini had fulfilled a long time dream after his retirement from the New York City Fire Department. He had scraped his acre of land in Greenville, NY with a *Rube Goldberg* device, a heavy, wooden frame, studded with many spikes jutting down. It was pulled by chains from a small, old, beaten up Japanese pick up truck. He could have hired a man to come in with a bulldozer for sixty dollars an hour and the job would have been completed in ninety minutes, leveling tree stumps, pushing large rocks and ripping up unwanted thorn bushes; but no, he was known as "The King of Field Expediency" in the Marine Corps in the South Pacific during World War II and enjoyed the art of doing jobs himself by makeshift devices. Making do with what he had on hand, had become his passion. It was not for the expense, but for the challenge.

The only problem with this last effort of scratching the ground and moving boulders with his little truck for three hours, was that when he went into the house for a drink of a cold mountain Artesian well water, and lay down for a quarter of an hour before he put the finishing touches to the 'new Sahara' he had created to the dismay of neighbors who had hung the wash that day . . . Pete died. Another problem was that Pete didn't know it.

He got up from the couch fully refreshed with the verve of an eighteen-year-old. Luckily his wife of thirty-eight years was out playing bingo with her friends that evening. He intended to go out and give Mother Earth another good going over. He felt like Edison and Einstein rolled up into one mega-genius as the inventor of his mechanical behemoth which changed the topography of his little acre. It had only cost him a dollar in the spikes he bought at a garage sale; the wooden frame was from an old bed and the chains were rusty, obsolete snow-tire chains from the garage, which he no longer used. He was still 'The King' he thought.

When he got outside, someone was standing in the increasing gloom near his truck by the Weeping Willow and the giant Norwegian Spruce.

"Who's that?"

"Hi, Pete. Remember me? I was passing through this neck of the woods and remembered you had a place up here. So I decided to check you out."

"Green? Richie Green? Motor Transport, First Marine Air Wing?"

"Yeah, how you been doing, Pete?"

"Good, good. I just retired, but I heard you got it on Saipan in '43."

"I did, I did, but I made out OK and I'm here now, right?"

"Right. How about coming in and having a beer and meet the wife later? She's out with her friends, but she'll be home in a couple of hours and we can have a bite to eat."

"Thanks, Pete, but I got to get going soon. Say you really leveled this land down with that thing. What is it?"

"I don't know. I just put it together because I bought those spikes and didn't know what to do with them, until I thought of this job."

"Still doing stuff no one else can, eh?"

"Yeah, I enjoy it. It's like solving a puzzle."

"You were the best, 'The King' we used to call you. I remember whenever we needed anything done, you'd do something. Like that two man travois to get Henderson and Black back to the field hospital. You saved two wounded guys, with one of them helping you. Henderson lost his arm, but you saved his life. I heard he went on after the war to become an Iowa State Senator."

"No kidding! I helped to save a future politician? If I had known . . . ," he chuckled.

"Then that P-51 that crash landed on Iwo and started to burn" continued the visitor. "Before the trucks got there, you and Charlie Wilson jumped on the wings and tried to break the canopy with some hammers."

"Yeah, I remember. We couldn't break that thing if our lives depended on it."

"Yes, but you did it with a .50 caliber machine gun as I remember. You blasted the top off until it shattered a hole big enough to get the pilot out before the Mustang blew. That was a close one."

"Yeah, I was scared. Later, I didn't think I would ever do that again. I was shipped out the next day on R and R. How'd the pilot do after that?"

"He didn't make it."

"Oh . . . ," he tilted and nodded his head almost imperceptibly.

"Yes, but his father heard about what you did and tried to contact you. You know, to thank you, but the old man died a month later. He wrote you a great letter though, but you never got it."

"How do you know that? You know a lot of stuff. And I heard from two guys that you . . . Richie stepped on a land mine and got it quick, so who are you, his son or something?"

"You're right, Pete, I'm not Richie. You were always too sharp to be fooled."

"Stop the horse shit, who are you?"

"Pete, you're dead and I'm here to bring you . . . you know, to where you belong."

"I'm dead?"

"Uh huh, yeah, dead."

"I'm dead, ha!" he exclaimed, feeling his chest and thighs.

"After all the work here and moving those boulders you took a blow inside and then you got a bad pain in the chest, remember?"

"Yeah, yeah, but I was OK after that."

The stranger shook his head with absolute certitude that was infectious. Then as he stepped forward, he put his hand into Pete's chest like a bayonet into a barrel of rainwater.

"God, how'd you . . . "

"Pete, you're dead, passe, kaput, gone, sayonara. I know it's hard to believe, but you'll accept it in a little while like most people. It's OK."

"The work, the boulders. You mean if I had not done that, I'd still be . . . "

"Only for a little while longer. You just pushed the time up a few weeks, that's all."

"That's all? That's enough. I could have . . . "

"What? What would you have done? You would have known, just like now and we'd have gone through what we're going through now."

"But, Doraine, my wife, what about my gran . . . "

"She'll be all right after a while, most people are. After the hurt, they start to remember the good things and tend to forget the bad. Your kids and grandchildren . . . the same thing. You did all right, Pete. You took care of them. You put bread on the table, raised a nice family as best you could, fought for your country when it really needed you. You did all right, Petey. What more can you ask?"

"Yeah, some of those guys were pretty young on the Islands. I knew one kid on Saipan who was just more than seventeen. His name was Mi . . . ," he broke off.

"Mikey Pendell," said the stranger.

"He must have been fifteen, sixteen when he joined up . . . Brave?"

"Come on, Pete. It's time to go."

"Wait a minute, wait a minute. Where am I going? I don't want to go any place."

"You want to stay here?"

"Yeah, why not?"

"You can if you want. I'll be back later when you want to go."

"Just like that, I can stay?"

"You'll change your mind. You can't make any more trouble for your neighbors, you know. No more dust storms and making of deserts when they hang out their wash. No more dragging cars in that you want to store and rebuild as classics. The one you brought in ten years ago, the little '62 Ford Falcon, was a classic episode, your magnum opus. Your buddies laughed themselves almost to life on that one. They called 'The King' again applauding, laughing, betting. I seem to remember a frozen rear wheel bearing, right?"

"Yeah, one rear wheel was locked up in a Long Island parking lot about two miles from home. My wife had to abandon it and take a cab home."

"And 'The King' got it home without a tow truck, right?" How'd you do it again?"

"I jacked up the rear wheel and took the tire off and," he began to laugh as he continued, "and rested the drum on a shopping cart and drove the car home at ten miles an hour on a Shop Rite shopping cart."

"The passing motorists' eyes must have bulged out, didn't they?" smiled the stranger.

"I guess. Besides, I didn't give a crap about them. I was worried that I didn't run into cops and get a ticket for something like obstructing traffic."

"I got news for you, Pete. The Suffolk County Police did see you and they couldn't believe their eyes. They laughed so hard, one of them peed himself. They made a bet among themselves, 12 to 1 against you, whether you made it to your destination or not. They stayed back far enough to remain out of site. Did you make it?"

"Yes and no. The shopping cart's wheels fell apart six blocks from my house, but I drove the car on three wheels onto my front yard scraping the drum along the ground. I made it, but without the cart."

"Yeah, those cops argued all day on who won the bet. Later, after almost coming to blows, they asked to be transferred to another cruiser, but they got over it after calling you the craziest names in the book. I'm sure you can guess some of the names. They never knew your best appellation though, *The King of Field Expediency*."

"Yeah, well I did it! It was one hell of a challenge and I enjoyed it."

"What happened to the car?"

"I put a new rear end in from the junkie, but it was a little different, bigger. It was from a Falcon Wagon. When I had the brakes done a year later, it cost me double because the brake shoes were different, bigger on the rear. So I had to pay for two sets of brakes. It drove the mechanic nuts until he figured it out."

"So you lost money."

"Yeah, but it was worth it."

"Especially to those cops," said the stranger. "They still laugh about it when they get together at poker games and tell the story to their friends. Your feat has become a minor legend in police circles on Long Island, Pete."

"Ha!" he laughed, "but I broke out even on the deal. Do you know a private detective came to the house a few times begging me to sell him the car? I finally did, and he towed it away on a hitch with a brand new Cadillac. I swear to God. A brand new Caddy! It's the truth."

"I know. Still want to stay, Pete? Your family and buddies are waiting to see you."

"I..., I, uh . . . "

"She'll be OK, I promise, but I've got to go."

"You're really . . . "

"Yeah, I'm him, but I'm more like a . . . , a friendly angel, sort of . . . you know how I'm depicted in books and movies and all that crap, a prince of darkness, carrying a scythe or hourglass and all that stuff. It's just Hollywood glitz, that's all."

"Damn, I'm going to miss her. I liked playing jokes on her, but most of the time, she laughed, you know? Hey, hey, wait a second. Look, I'll make you a deal. Give me those few weeks and we'll play a game of Liar's Poker with one dollar bills. We call out the serial numbers on what we may have on the bill and challenge the final bid . . . "

"Forget it, Pete, you used to cheat your sons when they were small and now even your grandchildren, memorizing the numbers on all the bills beforehand or not showing them your bill when they won. Besides, even if I win, what do I gain? Nothing. You've got to win or lose something on a bet. You know that better than I."

"How'll she find me?" he asked dropping his voice in absolute seriousness.

"Like you were sleeping on the couch," the stranger replied with a note of empathy.

"She'll be . . . alone."

"No, she won't. Your family's very good, six grown children, twelve grandchildren. Come on, Pete, how can anybody be alone with so much love around?"

"Where are we going?" he asked, steeling himself to the inevitable.

"Oh, we'll just take a little stroll under those stars over there, through your 'Sahara' dust field, and over that little hill."

"And that's it?" he asked.

"That's it . . . Come on, Marine, just one last hill," replied the friendly interloper.

As Pete started to walk with him, he turned looking back for a long moment and thought, half muttering to himself, "I should have rented a freakin' bulldozer."

SNUFFY, MY FRIEND IN NEED, INDEED

(Children's Version)

I hardly know where to begin about my friend, Snuffy. He's dead now and as paradoxical as it may sound, I'm kind of glad he is. I'd venture to say, speaking for him as I always did, he's very glad too. This is hard, and come to think of it, that's what he used to think all the time. I could read his thoughts when I was a stable hand many years ago at Belmont. I used to take care of him very well, see, and even though we became really good friends, I used to take care of him. You see, Snuffy was a horse. He wasn't exactly a race horse because he wasn't fast or big enough. He did earn his keep at the big stable that owned him. He ate the best oats and rye the same as Secretariat and Man-o-War ate.

You see, Snuffy was born on January 1, 1945 on a Kentucky breeding farm with good racing blood in his veins. For some racing reason, all thoroughbreds' birthdays are on January 1st.

But anyway, he was really all screwed up as a two-year-old. He came in dead last in the first five races they entered him in. Snuffy told me he ran his butt off with his legs churning at 44 miles per hour, which is like, phenomenal for a race horse, but his body was only doing 22. Gee, he even knew that a broken down old lady in a wheel chair with a flat tire could probably beat him at the wire.

Well anyway, Snuffy would never be in the Kentucky Derby and he knew it. Gee, and he couldn't compete in that kid's race with the wagons! You know, the Roller Derby or something? He'd still lose even if they put him in a big wagon going down hill with a push, a head start and secret pedals for his hoofs. I mean when Snuffy raced, it was like a Sam Peckinpaw western, where outlaws were shot and took two minutes to fall to the ground in slow motion or like the lovers in a movie running toward each other at the end when the hero can walk again and she's no longer blind after cleaning her contacts. Well, gee. You know what I mean. You know what? Snuffy was a realist, he knew his limitations and he accepted his destiny from the God of Equinox.

The next thing the owner tried, was using him for stud duty. I told you before, Snuffy had good blood lines and they took a chance on breeding him. They figured they might get a great genetic throwback like Carry Back or War Admiral. They tried it one day and brought in a mare in head named Kiss Me Kate. They put her in a stall with him but Snuffy had never been married before and he didn't know what to do, although he knew he wanted to do something. Man, the dope
just couldn't figure out what to do. He said he got this erection for the first time and it scared him and he thinks it scared the mare too. Well anyway, the two grooms who were there coaching Snuffy, pointed to the mare and simulated mounting her. Snuffy finally gets the idea and works his way on top of the mare.

Well, he almost mounts her and just as he's about to put the salami away for good, Kiss Me Kate kicks out, smashing into Snuffy's jewels with both hoofs. You could say it was he thoughts were no longer amorous. He says he tried to scream, but had no breath. He then tried to run away but his rubbery leg muscles wouldn't work. If he had the opportunity to lower his jewels into liquid nitrogen to stop the pain, he would have without the slightest hesitation. He just lowered himself onto his front knees and saw stars and sparklers for about twenty minutes in the hay. Soon, the head man came into the stable to find out the results and starts to curse at the two grooms. Well anyway, they took Snuffy away in a trailer because he couldn't walk. His jewels were swollen to the size of ripe cantaloupes. Poor guy was still trying to scream.

Weeks later, when he was healed, they tried to use him at stud again because he tried hard. Well anyhow, they bring him in and Snuffy thinks, if its Kiss Me Kate again, he would say Kiss Me Goodbye. Anyway, it's a different mare, named Token Rose, and she's much bigger. Snuffy looks at her monstrous hoofs and he felt a twinge of that pain again. This time the grooms don't have to simulate for the Snuff. They're encouraging and rooting for the Snuff. This time Snuffy approached with really meticulous care because he never heard humans talk about growing callouses or muscle around the "bells" and he didn't want them rung again. He wasn't about to play the part of Quasimodo again. No sir!

But you know how Mother Nature is so loving at times but, on occasion, she teaches a tough lesson. The Snuff really learned and he approached the new mare like a boxing champ. Yeah, like he had everything: speed, agility, deception, stamina, but no cups around his bells. He said he approached her with the experience and stealth of a champ, sort of forged by pain. He was instinctive, wary, watching all movements, especially the hoofs. After a minute of what he called plain fear, he touches her flanks with his muzzle and gets no negative reaction. He repeats the action with more force and still nothing. But the Snuff wasn't buying it, at least not yet. He said he'd spent too many long, long minutes on his knees in this very barn and it wasn't that he was praying. Even the ice packs on his bells hurt for the first week.

Nah, the new Sugar Ray of the equinox world wasn't buying any this day, sweetheart. He, like, feinted a mount and sprang back really quick. If Rosie had kicked, she would have missed, he thought, chuckling to himself when he was out of range.

Damn, he thought, she's either really ready or she was one sneaky mare. Maybe her name was Tokyo Rose. He had heard that name on the radio a few times.

He tried a different approach this time. He tried approaching on the left side for some reason which he didn't understand; jockeys and other human-like types always mounted on the left. So he tries another touch, feint, and fake mount, only the mount was at an angle just in case. Rosie laid a trap and kicked out. Snuffy did it again and fell back to safety out of harm's way. This time the mare lowered herself more. Snuff wasn't that big, you know, I mean high. I don't remember if I told you that or not. Well anyway, now he thinks, jumping butterballs, I might just get lucky. But, I'm still going to be sooo careful. I ain't putting my balloons up for auction, no how, no way.

He looks over at the lovers in the next stall. They had sat resting their backs against two piles of hay, watching. Snuffy thought he'd like a little privacy.

The exasperated mare whinnied really loud. She probably though he was a potentially gay stallion, I guess. His guard was still up though. He was going all the way. He was going to Shuffle All The Way To Buffalo. He approached, he shifted, he feinted, he touched, he half-mounted at an angle, he leaped off, he mounted on the left and then he finally grasped the prize and she didn't resist. Oh Equinox, Equinox! Thank you! She wants to get married! She loves ole Snuffy!

He heard the wedding bells begin to chime, but as he was about to consummate the vows, the grooms were yanking his halter back. They pulled the almost bridegroom rudely from the stall and tied his halter to the next one. Then they bring in Secretariat, after securing Rosie's hoofs to some leather boots stationary to the floor, and they put an anti-kick bar behind her, just in case.

Secretariat didn't make any touches, feints or maneuvers. He marries Snuffy's bride and retired to his broad loomed carpeted stall, with soft music piped in, until he's called on again to perform his arduous duty for the syndicate. Yeah, that's right, I said carpeted stall.

When I met Snuffy in 1950, he told me the story after I cleaned out his staff. Some summer nights I'd go to his stall and we'd talk half the night about life, liberty and the pursuit of happiness. Sometimes I couldn't sleep for an hour because of his talking about marriage and wanting a girlfriend. I wished we could have shared a cigarette or something, but he didn't smoke. We became pretty good friends. I confess, once I snuck him into a stall with a mare which I was sure wanted to get married or at least go steady. I really thought she'd marry the local rooster if need be, but boy, was I wrong. Man, she kicked the stuffing out of ole Snuff. His tactics were useless in the dark, but he took a desperate chance, something like Hitler winning the Nobel Peace Prize and accepting it in Moscow in 1943. He was unconscious the whole night. He had hoof prints on his neck, his chest and sides.

I never told him this, but the rooster dated the mare the next day. I really tried but, you know, the Snuff reminded me of my very nice Uncle Stefan. Great guy, but uuugly? He had only one eye and BO. One whiff would knock over a charging water buffalo. He couldn't get married either.

Remember I told you how I'm glad Snuffy died? Now maybe you can understand why. His luck was going to chance once though. He was going to be in a movie where he sleeps in bed with his owner, instead of a stall.

"No kidding!" I said, "What's the name?"

"The Godfather," he responded smiling proudly. Lucky he died before they shot his big boudoir scene.

Life is so hard! Come to think of it, that's what he used to think all the time. My friend, the Snuff.

STRAWBERRIES AND THE UNIVERSE

He rode down the stairs slowly on the lift his daughter had installed for his advanced Christmas gift. He had resisted the use of it at first, since he had little need of it but as time went on, it made his life more bearable.

"Good morning, ladies. What's for breakfast?" Doc Stafford asked as he put aside his cane and sat at the table grimacing slightly.

"Pancakes and strawberries, Jonathan, I made them myself," said his wife, Katherine. "Christine, pour the doctor his coffee, but no cream, give him 1% milk." His wife was still a beautiful woman in her late fifties, but the beauty was eroding like the tombstones in the Confederate cemetery nearby.

"What a beautiful crisp fall day to start a perfect weekend. And how're you today, Christine? How's your rheumatism?"

"Mornin', Docta Stafford. Ah'm still squeakin' and movin', movin' and squeakin'," said the hefty housekeeper. "How're you all feeling today?"

"Very good, very good. How's La Mic doing in school? He'll be home for Thanksgiving, won't he?" he asked.

"No suh, too far, but he's comin' home for Christmas," she said with pride.

"You tell that boy I said hello and I expect him to design us a new boathouse as soon as he graduates this year. I'll even pay for it, although he and Billy destroyed the old one," he laughed.

Christine served his coffee with heavy cream. She placed a plate for the pancakes and strawberries well within his reach as one of many minute repayments. He spread raspberry jam on the top pancake, then sliced strawberries and syrup.

"Why do you use both raspberries and strawberries, Jonathan? How can you get the full flavor of each?" asked his wife with slight annoyance as she sat down gracefully as if she were still being judged for her grace and beauty.

"I like both, dear," he said.

A car pulled into the curved driveway as multicolored leaves scattered from its path with its door slamming shut after the engine stopped.

"It's a waste, Jonathan. You could enjoy the other the next time I make them," she lectured.

"Katherine, I like both at the same time. In the great scheme of the mechanics of the universe, it won't matter one iota next year," he said.

"Really, Jonathan," she admonished her husband.

She was buxom, much beyond her own set limitations. Her make-up was perfect, albeit overdone to counter the years that passed since being crowned Miss Chayuga County in 1948. She fully expected to win the State crown thereafter, but she came in a devastating third.

Their daughter, Evelyn, entered the room carrying packages and a cloth shopping bag. She was six feet tall and slender. She had not a trace of her mother's fading beauty, but subtly had her father's warm craggy features.

"Good morning, all. Here's your yeast, Christine. What's this about our universe? Pop, have you been spouting cosmological philosophy again?" She kissed his temple and plopped down in a chair next to him. Christine brought a steaming cup of coffee with cream in it.

"It's just your father using raspberry jam with the strawberries. I never heard of such a thing. He should have used only one to enjoy it better."

"Mother, it's no big deal," she said, "Let the old codger enjoy himself."

"I knew you'd side with him. I expected it. Everything I say or do is always wrong," she said slamming down her napkin and leaving the room, covering her face with one hand.

"Catherine!" the doctor called out.

The silence started to press upon them when Christine left the kitchen and went into the laundry room shaking her head.

"So, are you going to take that promotion, Evelyn?" he asked. "It'll be a big step in your career with the bank."

"I don't know, Pop. It'll mean moving to Asheville and getting my own place. I can't commute from here. I don't know that I . . . " she trailed off.

"Listen, Ev," he interjected, "if your decision concerns us, don't even think about it. Your mother will be well provided for. You live your life. Grab it! I hope you get back together with Charlie."

"Pop, it's not that simple."

"I know, I know," he said, "but he could learn to get along. Even so, it shouldn't matter. You don't have to stay with her after. You two can live away from here."

"She can't make it without us, Pop. There's so little left after Billy . . . "

Many times she had seen him look away initially, although he visited the cemetery often. He had controlled himself so well through the many months. The only time she'd ever seen her father lose control of himself was the year after her brother was shot down over North Viet Nam. He threw a full bottle of brandy through his television screen after watching an American movie star smiling and aiming an anti-aircraft gun in Hanoi. Thereafter the liquor cabinet was moved to the next room.

Silence reigned again. He brushed back the side of his salt and pepper hair and took a sip of tepid coffee.

"Are you still sure about the operation?" she asked.

"Yes, Evelyn, I'd rather be in a wheelchair and lucid. I'm sure, believe me. Later, though, when it's bad again, I, uh, . . . I'd like you to know . . . " his voice dropped to a soft forceful whisper as he shook his head without finishing. He took another sip of coffee, then handed it to her to reheat it in the microwave.

He had seen much death and suffering in his life as a combat medic in Europe; tending the walking skeletons of Buchenwald; and later, as a doctor. He felt that he had survived the war and was way ahead of the game, so far ahead of his comrades and young dead German boys. He remembered fourteen year old prisoners of war released by the American Army on the promise that they'd return home, but many returned to the front lines to fight again and die.

"What, Pop?"

"Evelyn, please consider calling Charlie," he pleaded.

"Docta Stafford," said Christine popping in again, "Mizz Mills called this mornin' about her little boy. Ah told her you was retired and gave her Dr. Phil's number, but she insisted she wanted you, but I told her again."

"It's all right, Christine. Please call her back and tell her I'll be there soon. It's near the cemetery anyway," he said rising slowly, grabbing his cane.

"Yes, suh. An' Miss Evelyn, yo' bank called . . . Ms. Hervey . . . 'bout somethin' or t'other," she said and disappeared in the laundry room again after being surreptitiously waved off by Evelyn in helping the doctor.

She got his tweed jacket from the hall tree and held it as he put it on slowly. She noticed a pamphlet of the Hemlock Society in his side pocket. A few inches taller than he, she stood behind and continued helping him.

"You want me to drive you, Pop?" she asked.

"No, no thanks, sweetheart. Besides, I'm going to the cemetery later. I know how you feel about that. Then on the way home, I'll do a couple of wheelies on Old Man Turpin's meadow. He never paid me for that hernia operation, you know."

"I love you, Pop," she said as she hugged him.

"I love you too, sweetheart and your mother does loves you too, in her own way. Listen, do me a favor and think very seriously about what I said. Charlie really needs a gal like you."

"Yeah, right. I'm not exactly a new beauty queen, Pop," she smiled wryly with sensuous lips.

"There's all kinds of beauty in this world, sweetheart. Believe me, you've got tons of it. Some of it will never wear away," he said as she put on his soft tweed hat and tilted it to the side, which he straightened.

"You should leave it that way, Popsie. You look a little like Ronald Coleman in 'Lost Horizon.' You're such a handsome ole dude, Jonathan," she teased.

"I know, but I'm too short for you. Call Charlie, he's tall. Promise?"

She didn't answer as her eyes dropped and adjusted his collar, then walked him to the front door.

"Oh well, think about it anyway," he said as he ambled slowly to his vehicle.

She watched him get into his four-wheel drive International Station Wagon with little difficulty. It had served him well in the winter months traveling to the hospital and to homes when roads were almost impassable with snow or rain. The leaves on the trees had turned to myriad colors in late November with red and yellow dominating. The foliage was competing successfully against a vast azure sky.

The motor roared for a second into raucous activity, then quieted down to the tapping of valve lifters like sixteen woodpeckers seeking insects in the engine.

He waited a minute as the blue exhaust lessened and then waved to her as the wagon turned in the curved, dirt driveway and swung right down the road.

"How long?" she thought, "and how am I going to handle it?" Then she thought of Charlie's embrace and passion, then his demands and conditions. She turned back and went into the kitchen for her usual second cup of coffee. She reheated the pancakes and put on some strawberries and syrup and finally plopped a tablespoon of raspberry jam in the center. When she finished, she put the dishes in the dishwasher and walked slowly to the telephone.

DARK VIGIL

It was seventy-two degrees during the night in December. The guard duty section of Motor Transport, Third Marine Air Wing, came in a 2200 at the end of their tour. The pier had been quiet, except for the banging. The eight men came in silently, grim looking and haggard. The few who went to their bunks collapsed in mental exhaustion. After placing his Springfield rifle in the rack, one of them removed his steel helmet in disgust, slammed it to the concrete floor and bellywopped on his bunk with his crew-cut head buried in his arm. The others, waiting to take over the 0200 tour, seemed to take no notice. They felt the same way. The incessant intermittent knocking on the thick steel plates as they walked their posts, eroded their control. They had argued and fought over it for the past two weeks and were at the end of their patience. All had volunteered to work extra time with the Sea Bees. Finally, they were told there was nothing more to be done and they would just guard the dockside perimeter.

Private First Class Paulo Percini sat on his bunk staring into the void in front of his eyes, trying to erase the memories of this night. He had been a Corporal before he was busted in Shanghai for fighting three British Marines with knives with a wooden post. He had broken one's arm and sent another to the hospital with a serious concussion. The British commander complained, asked what punishment would be imposed. Percini claimed self-defense at his Court Martial, but was found guilty with no Caucasian witnesses to the melee and no knives produced at the scene.

He'd been stationed in San Diego where he'd met Meiko Orita, a young American beauty working at the Post Exchange (PX).

After a few months of dating, he asked her Japanese father for permission to marry her. Reluctant blessings were given. Her American mother, who also worked at the PX, knew of the hardships of being married to a military man, especially a Marine, whose wife had no chance of even unofficially following her husband to remote posts of the world. Had he been in the Navy or Army there might be major bases and ports for her to stay.

Her younger brother, Kimada, seventeen, joined the Marine Corps after graduation because of Paulo and asked to be assigned to Percini's unit as a condition of signing up. The recruiting sergeant promised it would be done after he finished basic training at Parris Island with that recommendation attached to his records. The squadron had been ordered to follow the main fleet to Pearl Harbor by the Executive Order of President Roosevelt.

Kimada came over to him at his bunk and said, "How was it tonight?"

Percini's head shook twice as his eyes closed to the inevitable question.

"Paulie, I can't take the duty tonight. I can't stand it anymore. It's driving us crazy. I had to hold my ears and I can't do it any more. It's the same with O'Hara. I'm going on sick call or just refusing and take a court martial."

"Are you fuckin' nuts?" he exclaimed. "Don't ya know it could mean the firing squad? This isn't a boy scout game anymore. We're at fuckin' war now! It isn't brig time, it's the wall. Sergeant Ederhardt won't accept sick bay excuses. He'll follow you up the Doc's ass if he has to and then have you court martialled faster than you could spit. There's only one more night of this shit, then we're transferred to reinforce beach defenses. Just one more fuckin' night, boy! That's all. Would you take twenty years in the brig, if you're lucky, for one more night of guard duty?" At this point, he was almost yelling.

"You don't get it, Paulie, I just can't take another night. I can't."

"Christ on a crutch! I can't believe my ears. Do you really know what you're fuckin' saying? Do you know what you're doing? What about your old man and your mother? What it will do to them knowing you've been thrown in the brig or shot?"

"Why can't you understand? I'm going on sick call. I'll jump off a building and twist my ankle or something, but I'm not going to listen to that again tonight," he said with tears welling in his eyes.

"Look, Kim, I'll request that we switch duties, OK? I know

Ederhardt from China. He owes me. Whatever you do, don't you report to sick bay or he'll howl for your blood. You hear me?"

He nodded.

Staff Sergeant Ederhardt stepped out from behind his cubby-hole quarters blanketed between lockers at one end of the Quonset hut. Someone yelled "Atten. . . tion!"

"Fall in by your bunks, shitbirds!" he barked. He was almost six feet, lean, with short wavy dark blonde hair. He wore his campaign hat with a partially shining Marine Corps emblem on it and a swagger stick under his arm pit. The end of it had a closed fist of carved ivory with the middle finger sticking up. It was custom made in Shanghai. It symbolized his thirteen years in the Corps.

"Point 1: An order came down from the Captain. We're to be out of here by 0600 tomorrow morning after chow. We'll be trucked out and set up for beach defense and patrol permanently. We'll be in two man tents until further orders. In a way, I hope the Japs don't invade our area and break through thinking how easy it was plowing through you candy asses.

"Point 2: It seems some of you haven't learned the meaning of obeying an order, especially now that we're at war. This morning while loading the revetment with ammo, I gave an order that the 'smoking lamp was out'! Later, as I pulled away with Gunny McCleod, I saw two of you shitbirds smoking. Those two jackasses, take one step forward right now!" he yelled like a banshee.

Three men stepped forward quickly, looking straight ahead. Two near each other and one down the far end of the hut.

Ederhardt walked slowly down the middle of the hut. His mirrored boots making the only sound. He nodded with pursed lips as he walked. He stopped at each man and looked directly in their seemingly unseeing eyes.

"O'Hara, cow shit from the Chicago! Ballard, elk shit from Montana!

And, of course, Percini, dog ship from the Bronx! You're so fuckin' stupid Percini. I didn't see you! You either, Ballard. I only saw O'Hara sucking on a butt, but I figured there had to be one more. The smoking lamp is now lit, gentlemen," he hissed pleasantly. One corner of his lips cracked a slight smile.

"Now the rest of ya, especially the newcomers, are gonna see some discipline applied to disobedience to an order which might save your useless asses someday in combat. You three fall in by my office on the double, now! Bentz, Hill, get three buckets and blankets. Put one of each near each criminal. Quickly, goddamn it!"

The two men scurried, ripping off three blankets from nearby bunks and securing three oval shaped buckets from an empty locker placing everything at the feet of the men.

"You two standby right here at 'parade rest'," ordered the Sergeant as he took out a full pack of Lucky Strikes.

He put five cigarettes in each offender's mouth saying, "Since you cunts like tobacco, let's see how you can handle five at a time."

He lit one each and said, "Now I want you to enjoy them," he cooed as the acrid smoke forced each man's eyes shut. O'Hara inhaled and tried to blow the smoke away from his eyes, hoping to outlast the punishment. Percini knew what was coming. The exercise had only begun. He'd been through it once before in boot camp.

"Put the buckets on your head and cover them with the blankets," Ederhardt said almost gently. In a minute, the coughing and wheezing were rampant.

"O'Hara are you still enjoying your privilege of the smoking lamp being lit?" he said as he banged on the bucket with the handle of the swagger stick, careful not to use the ivory end. There were no answers except the hacking coughs as each man fought against unconsciousness. Percini held his breath twice. Within a minute, Ballard fell to the floor and was left where he lay. O'Hara collapsed to a knee and held onto a bunk nearby, while Percini was reeling in place.

"The smoking lamp is out. Fall out!" he yelled and he disappeared behind the khaki blanket like a disdainful magician finishing his act.

* * *

Percini recovered himself in the night air after putting his head under the shower for ten minutes, coughing intermittently, trying to clear his throat.

Later, he knocked on the locker near the Sergeant's office.

"What piece of shit is knocking at this hour?" resounded the voice within.

"PFC Percini, Sergeant."

"Enter."

He entered, snapped to attention and remained silent.

Ederhardt pretended he wasn't there for half a minute. Finally, he acknowledged his presence, "Speak!"

"Sergeant, I have a request to make about guard duty tonight."

"Percini, what the fuck are you babbling about? Stand at ease. You just came in from duty, didn't you? Did that smoke burn your pea brain, Private? What the hell is going on?"

After hesitating, he realized it was a waste of time to evade. Ederhardt would get to the bottom of it anyway, as he always did. He was a bastard, but a hell of a Marine in anyone's book. Two weeks ago, he stood in the middle of the airstrip firing a .45 caliber pistol at a strafing Jap Zero coming right at him. Percini saw it with his own eyes from behind a wrecked PBY. He saw Ederhardt quickly reload and empty his pistol again as thirty caliber bullets from the Zeke spattered along side of him. He didn't even flinch. The Zero turned back and came at him a second time, but didn't fire at the cursing Sergeant. Instead, the pilot roared over him and waved his wings in admiration from one warrior to another. A bastard he was, but his steel balls played the Marine Corps hymn when they bounced off each other as he walked.

"Can I speak freely and off the record, Sergeant?"

Silence again prevailed as Ederhardt thought for a few moments.

"Go ahead, otherwise you'll fuck up again like you did in Shanghai, Percini. You should have been a fuckin' sergeant by now. Bu because of your big mouth and guinea temper . . . "

"Ernie, I gota take Orita's place on duty tonight. He can't take the knocking. He's gonna refuse or go to sick bay and I know you'll sniff him out and crucify him."

Ederhardt stood up in a flash. "That fuckin' Jap'll stand duty just like everybody else or I'll have him court martialled and shot. I'll request to head the firing squad myself!"

"The kid can't take it any more. He's only eighteen, for Christ's sakes, and he's not a Jap. He's an American just like you and me. He just heard his father and sister have to go to a detention camp, stateside. My folks don't have to go. I wasn't even born here, for Christ's sake! Your mother's German born. The kid's as American as anybody else. Give him a break, will ya? You and I know he'll probably be dead on some beach in a few months anyway, so what's the difference?"

"The difference is, fuck up, he's standing duty tonight just like the rest of us. How'd you think we all feel hearing that goddamn pounding every night since those fuckin' slant-eyed yellow bastards come in on us?"

"You can't blame him. Just let me take the duty. It's the last shift, Ernie. Please! The kid's a good Marine."

"Fuck, no! He'll be a dead Marine up against a wall in a few weeks if he doesn't stand duty tonight. Now get your ass out of here and I'll check on the roster and each man tonight myself."

"You're a fuckin' bastard Ederhardt! Ya always was and ya always will be. You hate all Orientals ever since you lost Mai Lee to that Chinese importer."

"Shut your wop mouth, Percini, and get the fuck outta here before I beat the piss out of you."

"OK, ok, asshole, let's go outside and settle this ourselves. Take off those fuckin' strips and meet me behind the latrine in five minutes. I've been wanting to play a tarantella on your ugly fuckin' poke marked face for months now!"

"All right, big shot, and if you win, I'll let you change the roster tonight. You can even bring your brass knuckles from New York if you want."

* * *

The shadows met behind the latrine and began their ordeal without any words. They fought long with fists and elbows crunching flesh and bone. One blow of a well placed boot to the ribs temporarily deflated one body cavity, but they continued until the kick was reciprocated to the shinbone of the other. Blood ran black in the brightness of the three-quarter moon. Breathing was labored to the point of unconsciousness. They grappled once going for each other's eyes, until a knee near the groin separated them. Finally, an uppercut by an elbow and a coup 'd tat of a fist to the back of the neck, laid one shadow low in the warm sand and unconscious to the world.

The heaving shadow standing above him fighting for breath, managed two words as it walked unsteadily away, "Guinea bastard!"

* * *

Ederhardt showered and changed. He went to McCleod's Section to have a few beers with other NCO's of the squadron.

As he was handed a cold bottle, McCleod asked, "Did that Zero come back and throw some anvils down on your face, Ernie?"

He just shook his head.

"Oh, behind the barracks, huh? Did you win or lose?"

Again no answer.

"I guess you won again. Well, gobble down that brew. It'll make your lumps seem to go down."

For the next two hours the NCO's guzzled beers, talking about future events. They listened to the military network on news of Wake Island holding off superior Japanese forces for two weeks, but most knew the end was near. Without reinforcements, supplies and food, the outcome was inevitable.

The newscaster reported on what the besieged Marines needed the most, "The response was," he announced, "send us more Japs!"

Ederhardt staggering back to his quarters like a drunken disorientated bee, fell down to the sand on his knees. He stayed there and repeated the sentence he had just heard a few minutes before, "Send us more Japs. What bullshit!"

"Wait a minute, wait a minute," he slurred to an imaginary person along side of him, holding up his index finger to a bruised cheek. "Sgt. Frutani's on Wake Island and he's a fuckin' Jap. How can a fuckin' Jap call for more fuckin' Japs? This fuckin' world is all fucked up . . . so fucked up!"

By continually changing vectors, he managed to make the back entrance to his quarters.

"Corporal Anderson, get yer female ass in here, now . . . Roy, get the fuck in here."

The Corporal came in and stood at attention in full guard uniform.

"Yes, Sergeant?"

Sitting on his bunk ready to collapse into temporary oblivion, he said, "Change the stinkin' guard duty roster. Percini, the guinea bastard, for Orita, the Jap bastard and tell Percini now."

"Yes Sergeant, Percini for Orita. Anything else?"

"Yeah, goddamn it, wake me at 0530 sharp . . . so we can get the fuck outta here . . . Send us more fuckin' Japs!"

"What was that, Sergeant?"

"Nuthin', nuthin'. Get the hell outta here!"

* * *

At 0545, as dawn loomed red in the east, the platoon formed and was about to load into trucks headed toward Mali Beach on the western portion of Oahu. Corporal Anderson reported all present and accounted for and saluted Ederhardt, who smartly returned it with a salty bent wrist.

"Private First Class Percini, front and center!" Ederhardt yelled hurting his throbbing temples.

Percini stepped forward from the second rank ran to the end of the second squad at port arms, then out in front of the center of the platoon, two steps forward in front of Ederhardt and saluted from the muzzle of the resting Springfield.

"Private Percini, reporting as ordered, Sergeant."

Ederhardt spoke slightly above a whisper without discernibly moving his lips or looking at him, "How'd it go this morning?"

"The knocking stopped. It was all for nothing."

Ederhardt nodded twice, "Yeah."

After long seconds, Percini said, "But at least, I got to bash in that ugly face . . . Thanks, Ernie."

He stepped back, saluted, turned and resumed his place in the platoon.

"By the squad, load up in each vehicle."

The small convoy slowly drove by the pier, where the now silent capsized California lay on its side.

The knocking inside had stopped, but unlike her dead sister, the Arizona, she would rise again.